GAVIN CORBETT

This is the Way

FOURTH ESTATE • *London*

First published in Great Britain in 2013 by
Fourth Estate
An imprint of HarperCollins*Publishers*
77–85 Fulham Palace Road
London W6 8JB
www.4thestate.co.uk

1

A catalogue record for this book is
available from the British Library

ISBN 978-0-00-747596-4

Typeset in Minion by G&M Designs Limited,
Raunds, Northamptonshire
Printed in Great Britain by
Clays Ltd, St Ives plc

In memory of my father

In the common course of things, mankind progresses from the forest to the field, from the field to the town and to the social conditions of citizens; but this nation, holding agricultural labour in contempt, and little coveting the wealth of towns, as well as being exceedingly averse to civil institutions, lead the same life their fathers did in the woods and open pastures, neither willing to abandon their old habits or learn anything new.

GIRALDUS CAMBRENSIS,
Topographia Hibernica (c. 1188, trans. T. Wright)

There I was now. In a room, a tidy room, tidier than any room I been in before. The bed was hard. The walls they gave no sound. A heavy window thumped itself shut. Good I says. Peace I says. First time I been in a hotel room though I was in an apartment once in the Canary. That smelt of bleach, this smelt of paint. I took in the room, I enjoyed it I did. I felt settled after what had been. I thought of the very nice girl in the hall at the desk. I thought of her the whole time I been in the room. I might ask her I says. I went in the toilet I seen they had not built the sink well but I came out in the room again I says I like this. I could live in this room I says.

When I got the call from my cousin Jimmy I went down to meet him in the hall. My cousin Jimmy was thirteen year older than me and he was my mother's eldest brother Thom's eldest boy. He was a bald man with gold teeth and tattoos on his hands and neck. We sat in chairs around a glass table.

He says are you liking the room.

I says it's grand. It's better than grand I says.

The business is appreciated he says.

No problem I says.

You know you're the only guest he says.

That true I says.

Did you see the picture of Raekwon in the bathroom he says.

No I did not I says.

You're in the Raekwon room he says. Every room's named after a rap star.

That so I says.

It is he says. But listen.

What I says.

Sorry he says.

What you saying sorry for I says.

He turned to look at the girl at the desk. The girl was watching television.

He says in a low voice you cannot stay here hear me.

What you saying to me I says.

He says some of the young lads in the town know about you here. They know you're in Rath in the hotel. They see you come cruising into town as chastisement he says.

I wasn't cruising nowhere I says.

Anthony he says.

I says there isn't no way they should see it as chastisement. Do they know who me mother is.

Anthony Anthony says Jimmy. There's no changing the way young lads' minds work.

Who told them I'm here I says.

Jimmy looked over at the girl again. Could have been her he says. The girls is worse than the boys.

And when should I leave I says.

Now he says. Tonight he says.

That bad I says.

There's fellas shouting your name in the town he says. We don't want this thing starting up again.

Sounds if it's already started I says.

Could have he says. I don't know.

Fuck I says. Where will I go I says.

He says I was you I'd lie low for a time. Go to Dublin.

I just come from Dublin I says.

Not your father's house he says. Go into the city of Dublin, go to a place they wouldn't think of going he says.

Fuck I says.

Serious Anthony no one needs this trouble he says.

I did not know what to think because Jimmy could be the fool what I knew of him but later in the night my mind was made up for me. The phone in my room rang it was the girl at the desk.

Is that your car out the front she says.

Mine's the only one there isn't it I says.

You better come down she says.

I ran down to the hall I couldn't believe what I seen. I seen outside my car was burning.

I says to the girl who done this.

She was still watching television she says I haven't seen nothing.

I ran out to the car I could not get near to it the heat. I looked about I could not see anyone. The hotel was a mile out of the town, all about was dark fields. I ran past my car I ran across the road in a field. I waited behind the hedge. I rang

Jimmy I says to him Jimmy you better get here and you better get me out of here.

I

1

I was thirteen fourteen month in a room in Dublin. More, even.

The landlord says to me the first day no parties no pets. The three Ps he put it but I waited for the third one and he never said it. That was the most words said between the two of us the whole time. I did sometimes think to keep him in a conversation for the mischief. He came in on a Thursday morning and you saw him hold his breath. He looked up just a glance this afeard look in his eyes and he looking at the corners where the black was spreading, at all along the lines where the walls and the ceiling met. He came in and he took the rent just got in got out the least amount of disturbance. I would laugh.

I don't know how much the other people in the building kept with the rules. I heard great noise many times. I heard twenty people falling down the stair, I heard banging through the pipes. It was a busy house but I would not see it being busy. What I know is there was the Egyptian in the next room. There was a man from Africa in the room the other side of the landing. There was a man from Africa in rooms on the ground. He had a woman from Holland and she was on the smack. They met in Holland. There was a fella name of Donie who slept in his shoes and he was in the room the first landing and he was from near Clare and near Tipperary. I think myself and Donie and then Arthur were the only Irish in that building my time there. The fella lived in my room before me was a fella name of Mac came down from the north of Ireland Donie said. I say it like I knew Donie but I did not. There were fellas from Poland three in one room but there were others from Poland as well. I seen a couple of Chinese too a boy and a girl. The fella was very tall. His people were from the west of China. I seen them once but I never seen them again, that was the way with these folk. But a lot of Africans all the time. It was just one of them houses. Other houses on the street you saw the Indians sitting on the steps or the Romanians but our house was one of the African ones whatever it was. Every shade you'd see. The women were not friendly but they were no harm neither. A man with sore eyes was in the university in Africa but he was in a gang and he got death threats. I did not know if this house in the city of Dublin was a good place to be hiding from people who wanted you killed but I hoped for myself it was.

It was an interesting house. It was more than two hundred year old. You would get the feel for it no doubt. Going up the stair, when I heard the noise of the floor board or got the smell of the damp, when I saw the lead in the fan window or the paint come off the ceiling, I got the feel for it. My room was at the top and the walls were not high but I knew of them in other parts of the house that were high. You could see the shape of the fruits and roses in the ceiling in the hall but you would not see the shape of them in my room. There was no carpet on the floor of my room, it was wood. When I moved my shoe on the wood I felt a grit. It was like sand or dirt. It had been there over the years. A man had come in from the sea or the fields, he had not taken off his boots.

I got information about the house off Judith Neill who was a lady looked after me who worked in a library. She was a Protestant. She gave me food and the things from her garden like radishes. She would give me tomatoes, apples and gourds. And one time then she gave me information about Public John Chiffingham. She gave it to me written down and it was something I was interested in. Public John Chiffingham was the name of the man who built this house. He built the street. Some of the food that was eaten in the houses in the street was saddle of mutton, a barrel of oysters, pike on a plate, the bird called the ptarmigan and marmalade tarts. The houses were turned over many times to many different people. For a hundred year the houses were turned over to the good people of Ireland. They used the wood in the house to burn to keep themself warm. When they were not burning fires they hid carbines in the chimney.

I met Judith one day one time I was depressed. I been in the house half a year, too long on my own. I was going mad, I went wandering. I seen a notice said this lady wanted people to tell their stories. She was collecting them from people like me. But she might think I am a strange one I said to myself, she would want me to slow down is what people say. I went to meet her in the library in the university and she gave me books to write in and books to read.

She said I should collect stories myself, they would help me tell my own. Would I not make it my business to know about the others in the house she said to me. She said those houses had many stories to tell. All the lives lived in them times gone by and all the lives lived in them today came to a lot of stories. In many ways they were the same what she said, the stories went on today and the ones went on before, they were all waiting for people to tell them. She said did I know the names of any the others in the house. I said to her Mac, the fella lived in the room before me. Tell me about him she says. I did not know this fella Mac, I never met him. I made up a story about him. Anyone with a Mac their name they were the son of a son of. This Mac came down from the north of Ireland and his father was in the gutter trade. I found a picture he thrown in my wardrobe of the Republic of Korea, I said to Judith he been going with a girl from the Republic of Korea.

Good says Judith.

She would ask me about my room, where it was in the house. Where she says and she went on like this.

At the top I says.

Where at the top she says.

At the front the top and the sun comes in I says.

Ah where the sun comes in she says. Tell me about the sun coming in she says.

I says it to her it's good because sometimes it's a sunny place. When the sun is out my room gets the sun. It's good but if there be a way to keep the heat of the sun that builds up in the summer over for the winter it be better I says.

Very good she says, like this.

Came a time though. After two month she seen she wasn't getting nowhere with me. I didn't know about telling tales. I didn't want to be snooping at people's doors in the house neither. A man who owned his own church said the wages of sin was death, nearly screamed his own room down. I didn't want to be killed, not by the Gillaroos not by no man for nothing. I was depressed all this time, it was a bad time. The air would get in on you. It was in the way things would come to you. The part of the city the house was was the place the whores were times gone by. The soldiers used come up for the whores. There were the pimps went around in charge of the whores they would lie waiting to hit the soldiers over the head who left without paying the night before. There were fellas too hid in the dark and hit the drunken soldiers on the head they knew had money because it was easy. The soldiers hid too and hit the men who hit them first. Holy men waited around to hit the pimps to get the whores off the streets. At any place you would turn you would find a man waiting to take it in hand the thing been troubling him. This is what you would think.

You could not be relaxed this time. Sometimes I would check. I would jump up I would check. I would be lying on the floor or the couch. I would be lying on the bed I would jump up. I would be sitting in my chair. I would go to the window I would check.

I watched from that window. People moved in the street, birds came up to the glass. I would see the spikes and wire, all around the roofs were forks. There were statues their face crusted in cack. Hello Saint Anthony I would say. I been told he was the saint of lost things. I did not know if it was Saint Anthony I was looking at.

This town had many corners. It was the thing I seen. The corners pushed you around but they would take you in. You would see the outsides of them, you would think of the insides of them. I had one of my own, a room hanging in the air. But you could not see it, you could only think of it. And you could only think of it if you knew it. They could not get me here if they did not know it, I said it to myself.

Other things I would think. I thought of the people done me down and of the people never done me down. I thought of the people in the library with Judith. I thought of them below where most the work got done in the library. The bowels of the building they called it, this lady Heather I met, an anorexic they called her. She said it was the bowels of the building and it was a good word. They were Protestants most them, all them, I got good at knowing. They never done me down was the way I looked at it.

I thought of the people on the street where there was a happiness was what you could see. I seen it for myself, I seen the arm chair on the road. I seen the tins of beer left about for whoever it was wanted them. I seen the childer on their bikes. There was one lad went about with thick gloves flattened all the broken glass on the tops of walls made it a safer place for the childer, I seen him. I seen the fella in the Ecclesiastical Metal Manufacturers when I was passing. He had the walls in the yard by the basement rooms painted yellow and he be sitting rags around him in his apron and the place filling up with the sun. I seen the Romanians and they were burnt looking and shamed looking people but not unhappy people, they were in fact joyful was a word that could have been used, they were a joyful people. I seen this one fella out with his trumpet on the street and he was good enough not to play it and disturb the neighbourhood but he was showing the childer. I asked him was it a trumpet, he said it was. They suited the sun the Romanians but it was difficult. The bricks in those streets were black, it was not a place that the sun could reach for long in the day.

I said I would give it a year in that house and I would see. But when my year was gone I says should I give it more time. I thought a year might cool it but I had no idea. The truth of me wanting longer though was something else. The truth of it was I was getting settled in the city of Dublin.

But you hear some things. People asking questions, people who go out in the field. The people who come to where the fields gather into streets, who follow the streets, learn to read them, come knocking on doors, going house after house, do you know this person, this person we are looking for, do you know this man.

Here are things this woman Judith Neill said to me. I was in her room in the library in the university. I was thinking of my mother, my father, my brother and my sisters. I was thinking of my uncle Arthur who was away distant places those days. I was thinking of the people been before us. Judith says you have to look at these things in detail and in whole and the story will make sense. I says is it fate you are talking about. She says it is not fate but from where you are looking it can seem like fate. Everything can only lead to where you are looking from and the more certain you are about where you are looking from the better to see what leads to it.

But I did not know where I was looking from but she said I should be glad to know where I was looking from because she was not certain where she was looking from. She was a woman sometimes you could pity and I think the Devil got in her if she had a drop. She had a man was sick with fits and was a weakness dragging her down. But maybe all these people had troubles like it I seen.

Judith gave me a cassette recorder one of the times. It was a box and it looked like a radio but it's a cassette recorder she says. She said it could be useful for me. She was standing in the middle of her room in the library her coat on and the room was a state. There were the carts packed high and there was paper on her table. I was sitting there I had this cassette recorder on my knee. The buttons had fallen off, they were now metal. I laughed I don't know why. It was because she had her coat on and her hands in her pockets and the room was a state. Only if you want it she says.

The cassette recorder is broken it will never be fixed but not long ago I tried buying blank cassettes for it. The man in the shop said to me I was part of a dying breed. I says to myself I am part of no breed.

2

Arthur rang me one sunny day the end of that summer one year after I landed up in Dublin. I didn't have his number put in my phone. I didn't even have it written down and when the phone rang I didn't know who it was. I thought it was Judith, I thought it was the juju man come to pay the wages of sin. I was in my room and I picked it up. I heard ah. It's your Uncle Arthur he says. Are you in trouble I says because that's what it sounded. He was breathing heavy through his teeth. He didn't know where he was he said. He was in Dublin and that's all he knew. He said he was at a Spar and there was a church near him and it was white and it had the babbies with the wings and the pillars and get here quick now Anthony he says.

The Spar I was thinking was a ten minute walk from the house. He was sitting at the window, one arm on a crutch the other on a bin. The head was over one side and his legs were spread out and he had the same brown face I remembered, the same thick hair, the same fat lips made you think he was whistling. He was holding a bottle of Club one hand and he been sick but not much. The sick was on his front and on the ground. He was moaning like the sun had got to him, he was moaning like he been boxed. The minute I seen him I says Arthur I says.

He says Christ Anthony.

I says Arthur Jaysus. It's good to see you I says.

Anthony I thought the kids were going to have a go he says.

I says who touched you.

No one Anthony it's me foot he says.

What's wrong with it I says.

Me foot and me head he says.

There was another crutch on the ground. The side of his feet was a dirty white sack said Mater Misericordiae on it.

He says Anthony can we go to your place.

Sure we shouldn't be getting you to the hospital I says.

No I just been at the hospital, they're useless he says.

They not the best people for this thing I says.

Aaah he says. Aaah. Anthony no. To your place Anthony he says and he threw the bottle at me.

Easy easy I says.

He could not hold the crutch on his left because his hand that side was in a cloth. He could not put any weight on his foot that side so I had to carry his other crutch and his sack and hold him up as we moved. Took us twenty minutes or more. I had to look at the ground the whole distance. His arm was thick and tense, it was a pain to lift my head. His hand in the cloth was up my face and it smelt and in my right ear was the sound of his hissing. I do not know how we got back to the house and up the stair. Inch by inch was the way. Counting brown metal covers in the ground, getting smaller and smoother and cracked the nearer the house, this was the way.

I got him on my bed. He let his crutch clatter to the floor. I let him lie, I threw his other crutch down, I says fucking hoor.

Where's me drink he says.

I put it in the bin after you threw it at me I says.

I got him water from the tap. Here sit up now I says. He was stroking his head like he was protecting his eyes. I put my coat under him.

Help me take me shoes off he says.

The left shoe was a struggle to get loose and I had to twist it. He pressed into his eyes the more I twisted it, I says you all right to him. Then it slipped off. The foot was bandaged thick except for the top where the toes were sticking out. Or they should have been sticking out anyhows only where you be looking for the big toe there was a mess. It was a state. There was no toe and there was blood, black hard scab and bright red blood. It was going bad I seen because there was green too.

What happened you I says.

I got in an accident he says.

You surely did I says. How long you been in the hospital I says but he didn't answer. I says how long you been in the hospital.

Shut up he says.

Don't be telling me shut up I says.

Shut up he says.

Don't be telling me shut up I'm only asking questions trying to help I says.

Shut up let me rest he says.

Shut up yourself I says. I says why didn't you ring me sooner I would have come. To visit you in the hospital I says.

Arthur I says.

Arthur I says and I smacked the bed.

Shut up he says.

I didn't say nothing, then okay I says.

I stepped back, I left him to it, I lifted my hands I says okay. And he was gone, spent.

It was funny, to go that quick. The things he been through I didn't even know. The hand stayed over the eyes but the elbow went slowly then the hand slid down and he was asleep his fingers spread over his face.

And there we were.

I tried to think of the last time I seen him and it was three year before, there about. It was in Melvin. Melvin, the Sonaghans, the Gillaroos, an old story. The colour to those days was black. That is what I was thinking. Everyone was depressed. And it was green and it was white because there were people after bringing flowers. Bright yellow too with the bibs on the guards.

And in came Arthur. He appeared, came out of nowhere. We all thought he was gone for good to France and England. But he came back these few days, his nephew being buried, my brother Aaron, why wouldn't he. The evening of the funeral mass we walked the fields around Melvin. I didn't think anything about them, they didn't mean nothing to me. These were the fields the Sonaghans and Gillaroos came from said Arthur, they didn't mean nothing to him neither. There wasn't too much praying done that night, only cursing. We cursed the Gillaroo boys that sent Aaron the threats on the DVDs. We cursed that Aaron had risen to it too. Arthur asked me where them DVDs were now, I said they were thrown in the attic. Arthur said they were evidence, I said they were not evidence sure hadn't Aaron killed himself. Evidence for what I said. We knew that the next day would be difficult. It was difficult. A very reasonable man said we had to stay behind a half hour in the graveyard and that made it more difficult. Arthur said to me were my mother and father all right with one another these days. I said they were grand. He said he was only asking because he seen them separated by the graveside.

He says how many of those people with your mother do you know.

I don't know too many of them I says.

He said to me he didn't neither. He said you wouldn't have known what was confiscated on the way in.

He tried to get talking to a guard but the guard would not say much. He asked the guard was everything okay and the guard said everything was good. The guard would not relax then because Arthur was looking about him. I was not sure if Arthur was messing or if he was agitated. He said the Gillaroos were fuckers and he kept saying it. He was jittering about, he was stupid, first time in my life I thought that. I thought Arthur you look stupid you are stupid. He was wearing a hat. I could not say if I liked it. He said it was made of felt and he got it in France. There used to be a feather in it he said. He took it down off his head and he showed me the inside.

What does that writing say he says.

He showed me his watch. There was mercury in it he said. He got it in Holyhead. He got his coat in England, his shirt in England, his shoes in England.

Where did you get your trousers I says.

England he says.

The priest said he wanted to speak again while we were waiting. He had trouble being heard over the helicopter but he got it out anyhows.

He says remember that Jesus was known as many things but one of the names he went by was the Prince of Peace. In the New Testament you will find a number of examples of Jesus greeting his disciples with peace be with you. Jesus's life was an example to us all to live our lives in peace and harmony with each other. We would do well to remember at this time the life that our Saviour led and the message of peace that he brought to us.

I seen my father make a great show of blessing himself. Then a guard came over whispered in the priest's ear. The priest said we would all have to wait behind longer. Ten minutes went and Arthur said he was going to throw a stone at the helicopter.

I'm going to try hit that thing and either I hit that thing or the stone drops and I hit a Gillaroo he says.

He tore a lump of tarmac the size of his fist from the edge of the path and he threw it in the air straight up. A guard stepped in and so did my sister Margarita.

Have you no respect for our brother she says to me.

I don't even know if that was the question. I don't even know if that is a question.

That was the last time, three year ago in Melvin, the time of my brother Aaron's burial. There was this time now he was after turning up in the city of Dublin he was agitated and there was the last time in Melvin and he was agitated then too. It was not good in the world when Arthur was agitated.

3

The next morning he took a turn for the worse. First thing I woke up he was groaning. He was not asleep but not awake. He was trying to keep himself through a severe pain if that's the way. His face had a clouded look and he was sweating.

I says to him Arthur will I make you tea but he was inside himself be the best way to put it.

I went to Mr L the chemist. He had the cure when I was sick in June and he was good. I says I have this uncle and it's like he's in the grip of something terrible. I says he been sick and now I think he's burning up.

Is he delirious the word Mr L used.

Yes I says.

He could have an infection he says.

I said to him yes that that's what I thought it was. I told him his foot had gone bad. Mr L said it sounded like it was the antibiotics he needed but that I had to get him to a doctor to get those. I said to myself that that was expensive and then I remembered I had antibiotics from when I got sick in June. I took one and I couldn't take the rest because the taste came off in my mouth. But I had them, I hadn't got rid of them.

I found them and it said on the tube take three a day. I knew there was no way Arthur was going to take them the taste of them the way they were, I would have to sneak them into him. I said to him did he want anything to eat. He said nothing only a groan. I had ham and I made a sandwich. I ate it beside him but he didn't react like he wanted food.

I left it a day. He hadn't eaten all that time, that day and the day before. I knew he was pushing himself to the limits. He would have to eat something and his body would make himself eat something. Sure enough when I bought chips and I put some on a plate beside him he took them. I pushed an antibiotic in one of them. He ate them down in ten seconds.

Have you anything else he says.

I got him an orange. I peeled it for him my back turned and I pushed an antibiotic in that too. He bit into it but his tooth hit the antibiotic and he spat the antibiotic on the sheet.

What's this he says.

I says it's a tablet it's good for you I says and I picked it up.

Give it here he says. Will you fill up me glass he says. How many of these a day do I have to take.

The rest of that evening he slept and most the next day he slept and the day after he was awake but quiet but together. The day after that then he was even better again, he was improved.

I was up that morning with the television on. I thought he was asleep and then I heard it.

Good to be home he says.

I turned to him. He was lying on his side, his head resting in his hand. He was looking toward the window.

I says you're not home. You're in my house here and it's my rules you're under.

And you're back now and you got sick and you're stranded in the city of Dublin and who am I to turn you away, one of my own, my uncle and the brother of my father I thinks to myself.

Home I says.

I says to him so what brought you back after your years of wandering.

He didn't say nothing, he let out wind.

Did you miss the country I says.

He moved himself up on the pillow.

Come here I want to show you something he says.

I'd left the sack he had at the Spar by the head of the bed and now he had it up with him.

Have a look here he says. There's some old pages they gave me in the hospital. Your father was telling me you're good with the reading he says.

When were you last talking to me father I says to him.

He came in the hospital visit me Arthur says.

Was me father where you got me number I says.

Yes he says.

Now he says.

Have a look at those pages he says.

Yes I says.

He showed me a group of papers, they were held together at the corner. The first page said in writing Recovery Guide for Patients Who Have Undergone Digit Replantation Surgery. The second page and the third page there were pictures. One of them was a man caught in a fence.

I turned the page and Arthur said the doctor got it for him off the computer.

Look he says, look, look, but I was reading down the sheet.

Look he says again.

I looked up and I got a fright. He'd took his left hand out the cloth been covering it and he was holding it in front of him. It was crooked and mashed, it was boiled. Took me a few seconds to see what was wrong. It was the thumb, only it wasn't a thumb. It was twisted on the hand, a different look to the rest, like someone had got it, broke it off, then they changed it, shrunk it, put it back on. His hand looked like a monkey's hand what it looked, like a chimp's. I thought of his foot and then I thought that that's what this was. That they took his toe off and they put it on his hand because his thumb went missing.

What's wrong with you he says.

I don't know I says.

Your face he says.

Your face I says.

There's nothing wrong with me face he says.

You look shocked I says.

It's not me face it's me hand is the problem, look he says.

He reached over for the glass and the hand stopped before it. It was natural a person would open the hand without thinking but Arthur was thinking. He was looking at the hand like he had to concentrate to open it. I watched him, his tongue tapping his front teeth. In a minute his thumb that was his toe moved back and he moved his hand around the glass.

I can do that but I can't hold on to anything yet he says. One step at a time isn't that what they say. I could try and pick it up but there's no power in the hand, the glass would drop. It'll take time. They had me doing exercises, opening and closing opening and closing. They told me I had to think through the movement and if I thought of it I would make it happen. They gave me fish they said the fish is good for the brain. They said if I.

The hospital, the doctor, the after what happened was all he was saying, I was not listening.

I says to him tell me something Arthur and tell me straight.

He looked at me strange, angry.

I says was it the Gillaroos done this to you.

He took two seconds.

No he says, and he kept his eyes looking in mine like a challenge what it was.

I turned mine away from his and I smiled, I smiled so he could see me smile, it was with no joy.

I says to him they must have thought you were good enough to let you go from the hospital before the skin is even healed.

He muttered something, I says to him what speak up.

He says I knew meself I was good enough.

You let yourself out I says.

There was nothing I couldn't have been doing on me own he says.

Can you do that I says.

What he says.

Let yourself out I says.

Course he says. They can't hold you against your will. And I don't like the fish he says.

Tell me this I says to him. Have you still got that watch the mercury in it.

No he says. That broke and it made me sick for a week. I got this new one with a wire coiled in it you could pull out and strangle a man.

Would you use it for that I says.

If I had to he says.

He looked around the room. I followed his eyes looking the way he was looking, this room he been recovering, this place he was hiding.

What you been doing with yourself these few days he says to me.

Looking after you I says.

What was that about he says.

Seeing that you weren't dying I says. Looking at you more than looking after you I says.

How do I look he says.

Bad I says. You stink. You're still wearing the clothes you came in I says.

Have you a shower here he says.

There's one down on the landing I says.

Will there be a queue for it he says.

All my time here I never seen anyone using it I says. I don't think they shower I says.

He leaned back crossway on the bed then rolled on his right and pushed himself up. It was an effort for him, I seen it.

Ah sweet fuck he says.

Relax there now I says don't be taking things too quick.

Ah that's good, that's good he says sitting up. Aaah he says.

Relax I says.

He sat there the edge the bed a minute his face settling into a more easy look.

Well he says.

Just sit there steady a minute don't be trying too much I says and he rolling his head round his shoulders. Don't need to be rushing to have a shower you're not that bad I says.

No he says. Then he says to me this, he says do you know where Grafton Street is.

Yes I do I says.

Good he says. He reached in his pocket his good hand and he had a bundle of money, must have been two three hundred euros.

Do you know where the Tommy Hilfiger store on Grafton Street is he says.

The what I says.

I heard there's a Tommy Hilfiger store on Grafton Street he says.

Where did you hear that I says.

I asked someone he says.

Who I says.

Someone on the street before meeting you he says.

You were fucking dying taking a turn I says and you ask someone where the fucking, I couldn't remember the name of the place.

Tommy Hilfiger store he says. It's a clothes shop. A big operation he says.

I says the only fucking operation you should have been worried about is the one they done on your hand.

Here he says giving me the money. Get me a long sleeve polo shirt large size. Blue or white or black or brown but don't get pink. And get me a pair of jeans not too loose at the ankles make sure. They do smart ones Tommy Hilfiger he says. I'm a thirty six waist thirty four in the leg.

Want me to get anything else with this money I says.

He reached in his pocket again pulled out another fifty.

Take this too in case he says.

Will I go down there now I says.

Whenever he says. Oh listen he says. Will you look out for something else for me. Will you see about getting me one of them wire camp beds. I wouldn't want to be throwing you out of your own bed. And I'm too sick to sleep on the floor he says.

This was too much to be hearing, I had to get out now, I had to do some thinking about all this.

I went for the door I says Arthur.

Yes he says.

Nothing I says. Then I says no I'll just say this.

I smacked the frame of the door my back to him.

What he says.

I turned I says I'll talk to you when I get back.

He says why you talking to your Uncle Arthur like that.

I stopped again I says no just tell me this. Tell me this. Are you worried about me kicking you out on the street. Because you can tell me you know. You can tell me the truth I says.

He says aren't you after getting awful big.

He looked at me.

I didn't say nothing, then goodbye I says.

4

Judith said to me to write because I am literate but I did not think of anything to begin. I did not understand and the truth of it is I wanted to forget it. I wanted to walk out of her room. I said I did not like the smell of coffee because I did not like coffee to drink. She said there was no smell of coffee because she was not allowed bring coffee in that room, she said that that was the smell of rotted paper. She said we could go in another room. The other room was brighter and had newer books and like the first room it had the marks of wood pressed in the concrete. She laughed at me she said I had more interest in the building than anything. Maybe that's your calling was the word she used. I said it to her I should have built buildings. She said no that she meant I should have designed them.

Then we started again. Would you like to talk to me she says.

About what I says.

Look she says and she took me and brought me the way we came. We went in a room beside the first one we were in. The books were bigger but they were brown and again I thought about the smell of coffee.

We're not going to stay here but I just wanted to give you a sense says Judith. She says think of all that these volumes contain. She picked up one book and dropped it on a pile of others and it made a clap.

We went out that room and we went to get water from a machine but the machine was empty. So then we went up the stair to get juice from a fridge. Then we went back to the room that was brightest and had the new books.

I want to tell you a story she says. We'll see if this sparks something. I want to tell you about the Lambton Worm she says. The Lambton Worm is a well known folk tale from northern England. It concerns as you might have guessed a monster. Some people say this monster had many legs on the side of its body and some people say it had no legs. How do you think it might have looked she says.

I did not know.

In the tale of the Lambton Worm a boy called John catches a creature that looked like an eel she says.

Did he catch it in a river I says.

Yes says Judith.

Then it was an eel I says.

John threw the creature down a well says Judith. The creature grew to a colossal size. Years later it slithered out of the well and terrorised the towns folk of Lambton. The funny thing is how the tale has changed over the years. The reason it has changed so much is that there are more spoken versions of the story than written ones. The story has versions even in other countries. In New York there is an urban myth about a baby crocodile that was flushed down the toilet by somebody who was given it as a pet but who didn't want it. The crocodile grew to full size even to an abnormally big size and lived in the sewers of New York for years.

Many times after being in the library me and Judith would get food in the university. We might go for a walk around the gardens of it. She said she could talk to the grounds man about getting me a job but I don't know anything about trees. One time we stood in the gardens and looked at the outside of the library. Judith said it was a wonderful and mysterious building. She said it was a puzzle the inside of it and it was a luxury but what it done for people was not a luxury. She said it was like a shelter, it was built of rock and concrete, it was a safe place. She says to me you should never be afraid of it Anthony. You are safe here you are safe in all these grounds, enjoy them. Enjoy the music of the bells she says. We walked over cobbles she says feel the smoothness of them under your feet, you can almost feel the smoothness run up your leg.

This one time she gave me a card. She said I could use it to get in the library on my own to look at the books.

But don't tell anyone I've given this to you she says.

Why I says.

It could compromise me the word she used.

I says what is compromise.

It would put me in an awkward position she says.

She gave me a book. It was a pad. She said did I have a pen and I said I'd get one. She said she wanted me to write. I was to go home. She said I did not have to go home straight away but I was to go home to the room in the house. She said she wanted me to write something down. To begin I had to think of one moment or a person. I must not try to get it all in she said. Just one moment or a person, and funny, I thought of Arthur. This is what I wrote.

Arthur has gone the furthest of anyone we know. He left in his van and he lives in it. Now I don't know where he is. He could be in Spain. He has seen things the rest of his people has never seen though there are some of us have travelled around as far as him. He is seeing mountains. He could be in France. He could be in Africa or China. In fact he has been to those places. What he does is buy things in one town and sell them on in the next. He sells bowls. He has sold winkles though he did not buy those. He sells films and he stripped a factory after the owner of the factory told him he could have it. He took all the metal and he sold it one place, all the rubber and he sold it one place, all the gold and he sold it in the other place. He took up a railway line sold that too. He sells food and antiques. He knows about the history of the antiques and the people listen to him. He can tell them when a thing was made and they will buy it knowing it is real. Wood in antiques is the thing he knows the most. He could tell you when a chair was made. One time he took a table to the top of a place where a man lived in Germany. The man said the table was worth a lot and Arthur knew that, he had taken the table himself up the stair. One time Arthur started a war in Switzerland. He went in a forest and there were no trees in the middle of the forest. He walked there. The men and women let a slab of stone thump to the ground and they had written on it they were going to get together and fight to be together. They needed one more man to write they should fight and that moment Arthur knew how to write and he wrote on the stone. They all shook their hand and Switzerland went on to be free. He moved to the next place. He went to Russia and he met their king. He went to the sea with him. He showed a town in Scotland how to milk a cow. They were not doing it right. Then they knew. He keeps on going. There are others of us has gone as far as him I know. But Arthur is seeing different things. The others go in a circle and always go back. Arthur just keeps going though he knows the way back. There has never been anyone done it the way he is doing it.

5

Arthur said the thumb was an accident what he kept saying. He said he got himself caught in a fence and his thumb came off. I said it to him wasn't that the same story on the picture on the sheet off the doctor he gave me. He said yes it was.

He said that that was why the doctor gave him the sheets to begin, because he had the same accident as the man on the sheet. Then wait he says. He got a text. I says to him who gave it you what does it say, I don't know he says. I says give it here. It said Greetings, still some appointments on discount days, Jizelle Hair Studios, ph zero zero zero zero one one one one one.

Did you try to get the thumb back I says.

No he says. He gathered his crutches then he put them down again. Then he shifted over to the sink, put water in the kettle. He says it's definitely getting better me foot. I can put the weight back on it and I'll be walking again no time.

Why didn't you try to get it I says.

What he says.

The thumb I says. It could have saved you and the hospital the bother cutting off your toe I says.

It was gone he says. Went in a ditch. Went in under the water he says.

And that was the leeches that had it then I says.

That was the leeches had it then that was it he says. Where is it you keep the tea he says. He opened the cupboard under the sink and the bag I had leaning against the door fell over and sweet potatoes I got off Judith spilt out. She grew them in her garden and I took them when she gave them. Arthur pushed down on one with his crutch.

What's this he says.

You cook them I says. But I don't know how to cook them. And they're five month old, they're rotted I says.

He got one up off the floor. But sure we'll try it he says. There's good eating in that.

I waited for the kettle to boil, I got up to make the tea. I waited for him to settle in the couch, me on my seat. I watched him. There wasn't nowhere for him to go out of here. It'd be easy if I just let things.

It's a grand enough room he says. A good bit of space indeed. Would you call this an apartment he says.

I took a sip of my tea. I will get this out of you and you will tell me you stupid fucker I says to myself.

So what's the plan I says. Are you just going to, and though I could not think what to say I sat back on the seat and fixed straight ahead on him.

He threw one leg over the other and hit the cup down on his knee. The bottom of the cup made a pop sound and some of the tea spilt on his trouser. Have you got any biscuits he says.

I have I says, I have, and I went to get them. I have Polos I says. Listen I says to him again. I want to know what plans you have. I says you have to have plans.

Oh I have many plans Anthony. Many many plans. I'm full of plans always he says.

You are to fuck I says, and I left him to it, I left him to it, forever at the tricks he was, all about the teasing. I felt like shouting there's no need to be protecting me Arthur, look it who is protecting who in these days, I took you in I fixed your foot I am feeding you.

I had a trick of my own. The trick was to get him when he was in himself. I seen these days and weeks sometimes he would get in a mood. I seen it usually when he had a cup of tea and a cigarette and he was sitting on the single wooden seat. He would have his legs crossed, he would have his arms crossed, he would be bent over himself. There would be steam rising one side, smoke rising the other, his head would be lowered, low as his shoulders. He would be looking at nothing. In this mood you would not get him telling you things straight but you might get him telling you stories.

One of these times I was looking at his hand with the cigarette in it, his buckled left hand. His thumb that was his toe was pointed the wrong direction, it brought out my pity, I expected it he would start whining and whimpering. This moment I did not want this beaten dog, not this thing his hand and foot buckled and broken. I says to him I'm sure you have things on your mind, you cannot be a travelling man you don't have things on your mind the next place you're going I says, and I said it to lift him make him feel like a man with things on his mind.

I says you must have known some stories your time on the road.

Yes he says.

How long were you away I says.

I don't know he says.

I'll tell you what it was I says. You were five year away. Two year before Aaron's burial, three year after.

Was it that long he says.

It was I says. I think I says.

I says would you like a drink, I have some in the room.

What have you got he says.

I went over to the cupboard on the wall. It was screwed on the wall in the middle on its own and the latch had turned green. The only thing in it was a bottle of xeres it said on the front. I never touched it before this time. I twisted the cap and it ground on the glass with the crust the inside of it.

Have that I says, the man lived here before left it behind him, it is drink for the road.

It was the evening, it was one of them evenings after a clear day that the mist had come down catching and spreading the light wide through it. Arthur sipped at his drink and then I seen him sniffing his shirt.

I says something wrong.

He says my shirt is smelling of smoke since I came into Dublin.

I says I am used to it. Is it cars I says.

That's what it is he says.

Cars and damp and electrical heating I says.

Reminds me he says.

Of what I says.

He says reminds me seeing Dublin years gone by standing the top of the hill of Kitty Gallagher and seeing the smoke bedding in in the evening. It was the damp of the air kept it down. The smoke every chimney would collect and the whole of the town be smothered in its smoke but you don't get that no more because they banned the coal that smokes they did.

Have you any more stories I says to him.

He lit up another cigarette and smoked it quiet to himself, sipping slow the xeres and his eyes squinting.

He told me the story of the alms badge. This was the story.

They used give out the badges made of tin to the beggars of the city of Dublin and our people heard of it he says. But only a certain amount of badges was given out, only a small number of the beggars was allowed get a spot in the city to beg for the alms. Anyone else wasn't allowed. So our people heard of this and in them days they were out beyond the last ditch, what they called the franchises, where the men who ruled the city every year would run out with their horses and set the limits of the land under the city and our people was on the edge of this. But one of our fellas Brackets Sonaghan took it up with one of their fellas he says why don't you be giving out the badges to us out here. But the rest of our people says to Brackets why you saying that, we are earning a decent living working for the yeomen garrison, and it was true, we was it was said doing the work for the yeomen helping out with their tack with their utensils and their weapons. This lord who rode out he says to Brackets you have to be living in the city and you have to show yourself to be a beggar and he had a friend with him and they says sure we'll show young Brackets here what it's like to be poor and no shoes in the city. And they took him aside, they took him to some trees, and they gave him drink like this until it was dark and they had a fire lit and they were telling tales and getting each other spooked but it was only to get Brackets over to their side for the night. When it was midnight and Brackets was drunk and relaxed they done something terrible to him. They put the pitch cap on him and Brackets was in agony. They put him on one of their horses and the lord's friend took Brackets's horse and they followed in behind Brackets whose head was on fire. The horse Brackets was on knew the way back to the city and the lads were behind shouting and whooping and following this ball of fire that was Brackets. But when Brackets's horse got near the city the fire went out and Brackets was able to concentrate on the horse not his head. He was able to turn the horse into a field and the men went on straight didn't know where Brackets had went. Poor old Brackets fell off the horse and he cooled his head in the swamp that was in the field. When he woke up the next morning he seen that in the field was a fair being set up, all the tents, the ovens cooking the chickens. The people in the fair they took pity on him because his head was black. A man with a tent said he would give Brackets a cut if he sat in the tent and let the people come in and look at him. Brackets did this for a week and then he was off but he said he would go in the city because he was so near to it. And in the city the people there took pity on him too because of the state of his head. They gave him money though this was not allowed because he didn't have the alms badge until one day a gentleman said to him he should go to the town hall ask for a badge. So Brackets went up to the town hall, he knocked. And do you know who opened the door to him.

Who I says.

The lord the fella set his head on fire. Course he did not know Brackets to see now and he gave him the alms badge. But what happened him then was Brackets got so good at the begging the other beggars turned on him. He got a good amount of money this one day he was able to pay a man to take him all the way out of the city back to our people. When he got back to our people he had to tell them he was Brackets Sonaghan because they did not know him to see. They said to him where he been these years. He turned out his pockets and he showed them the money he had and he said he been a very successful beggar. He showed them the badge made of tin. He said it was easy. They could make these badges easy, if anyone could it was them. He told them he had the best meals he ever had and he been taken in plenty people's homes in the city. He said if they took the tin they got from the yeomen made up a load of these badges they could go begging instead of this skittering around the yeomen. But you know what our fellas said.

What I says.

They said they weren't going to go down that road. There after been a barracks had been set up near enough and these fellas had taken over from the yeomen and they were from Cornwall in England. And these was fellas who worked in the tin mines and their people worked in the tin mines and these people could see the work that our people were able to do with the tin. They appreciated the skill and they made our people proud of the work they were doing because they said it. So our people said that was it. They said no to Brackets Sonaghan and fucking matchstick head was put on his way.

Fucking matchstick head was put on his way he says. Was good he says.

I says to him what would he have done. I says would he have gone along with Brackets or stood with the rest of our people.

Arthur said he didn't care because it was only a story.

No man would survive his head being set on fire he says. He be dead before even being put up on a horse he says.

That is true I says.

He says I'll tell you something about that story though. What's true is them fellas from Cornwall in England know it all about the tin. I been there meself. There is tin mines the length of the place. Not too many them left open now but I met these fellas said their people worked in them. They took me in said I was their brother they told me.

Arthur threw his head back laughing the thought of the word they used.

He says they were going to march on London they said. But first they wanted to drink. I spent I say five month there. Most I ever spent in one place anywhere in England.

What kept you there I says.

I was relaxed he says. I watched the fellas on their surf boards on the water. I slept on the beach a lot. I got a batch of this sex wax they called it and I sold it to them. Then I got another batch and another. It was for their dicks on the surf boards. I could have gone on. And I was with this woman. I met this girl I had her one night on the beach.

Arthur finished off his glass the xeres one go.

No more of that he says. I shouldn't be telling you things like this.

I could feel me getting drowsy, I could feel the heat of the lamp on my lip.

I says Arthur you've a gift do you know.

For what he says.

For setting out the story there in front of someone and the light and life in it is there to see. It's a gift no doubt I says.

A thick moan blew out in the night and came in through the walls. This would happen.

Sh what's that he says

I says that's the boats come in on a misty night Arthur all that is. We're only a mile or less from the port and that's the fog horn alerting the other boats.

He went over by the window looked out as if he could see. He was stood there his good hand in his back pocket, the bad hand holding open the curtain.

Gone to see the world he says.

I says they are.

They can keep it he says.

He looked above him then, his head moving with something.

And what's this come here he says.

I went to the window. Two strokes of light were moving through the mist. They were settled on the thicker cloud above and the spots they were making were moving ten mile across, back to touching, out again.

It's coming from the port too I says. There's something always going on out there I says.

We did not like to look at it too long. I poured out the last dropeen of the xeres.

And musha musha have you a story to tell yourself for your old uncle little bookaleen he says the night getting on.

I went over to put on the television.

I don't know fuck all about stories I says.

6

Here is a good one. Judith Neill tried to sink a submarine. This was a long time ago. A submarine of the Canadian Navy was pulled up in Dublin for show. Judith went along with some old friends to try gather intelligence is the word. Never again she said. She said she'd left that person she was behind in the past but she was fond of her all the same. She had a tattoo remind her of times gone by. It was the head of a fox, on the inside of her arm near the elbow. She was trouble back then she said but she was lucky because she could have been in even worse trouble, she had got away with it. I said to her I would not tell anyone about the submarine. She said to me I could tell who I wanted.

She said this the first day I met her. This was six seven month after I came to Dublin, five six month before Arthur came. The first day too she said to me questions about my mother. She said to me what was her hair like. I had not thought about my mother, I could not think what her hair was like. I could only go away and think what Judith was like because she was the last woman I seen. I thought she might have been a young person, then I seen the tattoo gone blue on her skin. But the skin sat on her softer than on my mother was what I thought. My mother had hard skin with white cracks.

I could think of my father better. I said to myself things. I said Aubrey Sonaghan was a big man, bigger than me. I said Aubrey Sonaghan had black hair, Aubrey Sonaghan had dark skin. Aubrey Sonaghan had brown eyes. Aubrey Sonaghan wore brown. Aubrey Sonaghan wore a brown shirt made of the same thing a towel is made.

In the university I bent down and touched a cobble in the ground. It was smooth and cold like the top of a skull.

Aubrey Sonaghan is still alive I says. And why wouldn't he be alive I says.

I said it to Judith.

My father is still alive I says.

She says it too, why wouldn't he be.

But had I not made it easy to see. This man had laid the lines in himself that would kill him.

The king with his fists, the champion of Ireland, I had written before, the picture I had of him. It could only have been a picture because I do not remember him the champion of Ireland. The picture was the dust on him in the blood. Or the muck and the steam on him, the muck of the fields, the slugs, this man standing in the middle, the mist. He put down anyone came to the fields to take him on. The McGlorys and the McInidons, Kim Jonah come over from Manchester, Driver Fournane from the west, the Saltman Vennace. And anyone the Gillaroos put up against him. He went through them all, beat through them because they came in his way, roads and paths of blood and muscle and bone. I used think it was not pride kept him going. All the others it was pride brought them to him. But I thought that if it was pride in my father he would not have given up. He would not have given up the fighting and he would not have given up his ways for the settled life. Then I thought about it there is two kinds of pride. And it was pride in his person made him stop. He backed out the fighting right at the top, he was unbeaten. And he put away the other pride to back out, to go a different road. There is a pride in your person and there is a pride in your people.

Not all of this I had said to Judith. There were certain things she didn't want to be hearing, I learnt that early. She didn't want to be bothered with no one's troubles. For two month I been coming to this woman's room the top of the library, I been getting the food, sometimes money.

Your dole has been cut she says to me.

How do you know I says.

I read about it in the paper she says.

I seen a thing on the television the couple of nights before, I didn't want to say a thing. Damien Thresh Sonaghan Lee a fella twenty eight year of age had went missing near to Galway and they didn't know if he been kidnapped but then they knew he was kidnapped because they found him after the week lying dead in a lane drowned with white paint that was tipped in his lung.

You look tired Anthony are you feeling well says Judith.

But of course I was not feeling well, I had not slept well the last two nights I was sick thinking. But the Sonaghans and the Gillaroos and their feuding and fighting for hundreds of years, they went on in the world this band of wise people and singers dancing in this woman's head.

You heard of this fella Damien Thresh Sonaghan Lee I says to her.

No she says.

The fella was found dead drowned in paint in his lung I says.

Oh no yes I had heard about him she says. Was he related to you.

Only distant I says.

Oh dear she says. It is brutal what goes on she says.

It is brutal it is true you are right I thinks. And it is brutal how it all comes close. Came as close as it gets the night before, I went to bed thinking of Damien Thresh and his head held, soon I was thinking of my own head held. The doctor been around to our house when we were childer, got called in the middle the night because myself and Margarita were sick. The doctor said I must drink milk but I would not drink milk. Margarita would not drink milk neither when she seen me sick with it.

The doctor is a man knows more than you my father says. Same time he's saying it his hand is swinging taking me by the hair, holding me to the table. Same hand that would hold my mother to the table, would hit her in the rib.

I been clicking my fingers all the night and in the morning before coming in the library.

Judith says to me you are a gentle soul Anthony.

I would not stand for it I got up out my seat I went to shout at her but I said nothing.

I sat down again I got back up. I went over to her I put out my hand I says are you okay I wasn't going for you. I took my hand back in again. And that morning I been walking up and through my room clicking my fingers thinking how quick my father could turn, the change in him.

I was thinking foolish woman.

She says Anthony it's okay.

I says sorry for this do you know who I'm like is what it is.

Yes yes leave it it's okay she says but she did not look okay with it and now she would not talk.

Now we sat in the quiet until things were calm. And it was strange, sitting there now, in this room with music playing, a strange music. I heard something like it before but not this music, it was classical music she said. It was a thousand old airs at once. It sounded like wind, it was music for the mountains. I looked out the window I seen the water twinkle in the sun on the grass, I seen the clouds rise six mile, it was music suited that. It was a moment like this with music like this one of the wet sunny days I thought what my mother's hair was like, it was like the dead yellow blinded summer grass.

But it was strange now all coming to an end, me and this woman Judith, and thinking of the danger coming. This building it was said was a safe place would turn me out I was sure. Turn me out into the streets where sure too would be my fate, I would meet it, boys with hooks and knives scraping them on the ground smiling. I was waiting for it listening to the music, listening to the people in the library coming and going. People were saying things to me. Strange types, different people, good people and friendly words, it was not real. A woman name of Melissa said her dogs were her flowers, that she would lose herself in her little puppies like falling into flowers, a man name of Roy, saying questions for jokes, a man name of Professor Michael Gregory, stopping by Judith rubbing her back, though no words were said about her back, she rubbing his back and saying to him are you all right today, is there any point in another referral, the two of them talking these words in front of me though I am there, and I knew it all now this change in the air, it is what happens before I am to go my separate way.

But I've just bumped into RB I had a chat with him says Professor Michael. Twenty minutes we were talking, the years just rolled off, him and me.

Judith says sometimes I think you are too old for me Michael.

And suddenly we were back in our little Tangier says Professor Michael. It was like the golden days. We said we would have a bottle of wine in the Bailey. Maybe I will smoke something illicit or maybe I will have that dinner in Jammet's I've always promised myself. Senex bis puer.

Stop speaking in tongues she says.

Oh where is your Latin dear he says.

He ran back to Montevideo she says.

I listened to that music. It could hit you in the eye and take your head off. You could fall asleep to it. You could eat a very grand meal to it or it would fill you with the power to lift a weight. I looked at the clouds rise to the six mile. In front of the clouds I seen the sea gulls swirl around watching the ground. I expected one to drop out the sky make a go for it any moment. I seen a sea gull my early days in Dublin do that. He took up a slice of pizza from the street had black marks on it, he shook it like a cat with a rat, he swallowed it one go. He got forty feet in the air and he came down. There was a crowd of people looking at him on the bricks of the street and he was two blue sacks and a ring of feathers was all was left.

There was a quiet now in the music would make you do something.

I says to Judith but you know my father had ideas.

Judith looked up, this testing face on her, she was working on fixing a book.

I says he had ideas to bring up our family the best way he could, to raise us up in a house was normal.

Of course he had says Judith, everybody has that ideal.

This I thought this moment this time sitting in the sunny room the top of the library. I thought there wasn't no one should have abandoned my father because of his ideas, not my mother the dead grass hair on her not my sisters not no one.

In a house that was normal, with settled people about I says. Our people that are in houses live surrounded by others are just the same. My father took us all into a house away from that, in among houses with settled people. People said things and people laughed at him. People hated him they did. But I can see it now he was right to be thinking this way I says.

I pressed my knuckles down on the back of the radiator, felt the heat in my hands, pressed the grille in the heel of them.

I says I see the people about me now in this city, I see the people in the university, and they are good people, my father was right.

I started laughing.

I says sure amn't I a settled person meself.

You keep talking about your father as if he is dead says Judith. You keep saying was. Where is your father now she says.

He's keeping on the way he was set I says. No reason to be thinking or saying anything other. He might be dead and gone and twisted to smoke but he might just as well be sitting good decent people from other settled houses around him talking about things. He might be enjoying a drink with them. He might even be living in Spain all I know, with land down there all I know.

Judith had stopped working on fixing her book now. She was looking at me, she was thinking. She said to me she wanted to help me out any way she could.

Even a little she says.

She gave me an envelope, two hundred euros in it.

Your bonus the word she used. And for all you've done to help me these last couple of months she says. You know my door is always open.

And this is it now I says to myself. Out now in the world again after letting her down, after showing my teeth.

Her phone rang, she was on it five minutes. She did not say much to the other person. Will you she kept saying. You will be very comfortable. I think stress brings them on she says.

She got up and she said she was going home.

I am sorry I says to her.

She didn't say anything, waited for me to say more.

I says sorry I couldn't be the help you wanted.

Anthony you've been just great she says. She put her arm around me, she pressed me in against her. I laughed, then I went cold.

At the canteen a man in black had to let me in around a rope. He said I could have my dinner but I'd have to eat quick because there was something happening later. I watched the few people were there, a priest in a grey suit, the older people it was said had come to the learning late.

Many ways I was as well to be away from Judith. I did not like that she was out to touch you, I did not like the way she put on the soft voice. It would compromise you it would. You would feel like a fucker if you said anything against this. And I did not like the feeling all I done was a waste of a person's time. I didn't want to be leading her think I am a person I am not, and now I was left like this. Left I didn't know where. In this place with low ceilings Judith said were vaults. Left with I didn't know. Two hundred euros. Left with thoughts. I thought of the things I been through. I thought about what I should do now. I would be taking the dark streets back to the tall house over the river soon and I did not think about the dark in them streets for two month because of what this woman Judith done for me.

I thought about my father. I thought about the good things in him. His ideas. I thought he was not vicious with animals. I will say that about him. There was a horse the end of a field one Sunday near the house we lived, he could not see it being hurt. It was drinking from the pipe and it was bet up. There were sores on its neck and flies were drinking from the sores. My father went in the field and he led the horse by the head out the field. The boy who bought the horse stopped him on the way says it is mine and my father said to the boy where he get this horse. The boy said he got it in the Smithfield market. My father made the boy sit up on the horse keep it in control and my father walked beside it touching the horse's head saying kiss kiss horsey horsey. They were going to walk back to the market, there was an hour left of it. My father wanted to sell the horse to a better owner see its condition would improve. He did not care who he looked like he just wanted to see the horse was okay. People seen him and he seen them seeing him but my father walked in the roads and streets, he was not thinking about his ideas to be a settled man he was only thinking about the horse.

But I got a phone call from the guards say my father was in the station. They took the horse from him and the boy and they gave it to the horse group was what they said to me. When I got to the station my father was singing quiet no way no Botany Bay today. Outside on the road I says to him was that all you could say to them people. It was said my mother's grandmother died in a station in the north of Ireland, they wouldn't leave her alone. I says it to my father this would be the same men that would kick the fires and move you on. I was angry with my father. I says they wouldn't give no reasons to interfere. You have no pride I says to him. It was true, he had no pride left, never in his people, now not even in his person. I let him go on ahead of me to the car. He had grey dirty sheets flapping from his back and his shoulders were wide as a wall. He stopped, he turned his head to the side to say something, I stopped too. He was a slow sunken beast was how he looked. I waited until he went on again. And there was nothing until we were in the house and then dominay dominay dominah started, his words to God to beat him.

In this empty canteen with the women cleaning up the dishes I thought about where to go and I says I will stay where I am until I am cleaned up too.

7

This is not something I said to Judith. This is something I am saying now. The time I am thinking my mother had not left the house yet. That was years away. My brother Aaron was alive this time. He had a good few years to go. He was twelve,

I was ten. My sister Margarita was eleven. My sister Beggy she got called though her name was Kate the same as my mother was eight.

The house is miles from the country. This is Dublin, we were Dublin, but we did not go to Dublin. We stayed in the house and we went down the shop for milk. We got on the roof, we worked in our garden. We fixed our car and we cleaned words off the door of it some boys put there. Some boys wanted to get me back for hitting them and they sat on our wall. Their daddies came and stood for a while. My father went out to speak with them and he shook their hand. You could not call these people country people though there is some that calls them country people. There is some that calls them buffers too though that is not a word I have known. My father did not use the words like buffer. My mother I think wanted to get out. I do not think this I know this from later. She wanted to be with her family that was out in the world. She wanted some day to be with the tall white stones of her dead in Rath.

My mother was happy to see her brothers come to the house when my cousin Paul made his communion. My father respected this and he gave Paul money. But he did not like my mother's brothers because he knew they didn't like him. They have come to the house as a message or a warning he thinks. They lived in houses too but it was different. They lived in houses were surrounded by their own. They did not like the Sonaghans and never would, it was natural. And they did not like a Sonaghan had moved to a house like this in a place full of buffers. They said the word Aubrey like they were playing in their mouth with a stone, the same as the word buffer.

Do you still do the fighting one of them says.

My father did not answer, my mother did not speak for him. My father moved around my mother's brothers in the kitchen or he stayed watching the television or he went in the garden to work on the fountains. He made fountains. He wore gloves doing it because of his psoriasis of the skin. I heard my mother's brothers say is he still making fountains. My mother says leave him to it and she was laughing. Her hand was holding up her head and she left a pot boil up for her brothers until the window was misted.

My father made great fountains. That is the one thing the people in the estate knew about him. He made a fountain for a man and a woman with a nude woman lying across the side. After this all them on the road wanted fountains with nude women lying across the side. He will do you a deal they had said about him. My father made a fountain for my mother after they got married. It had a nude woman but it also had a nude man on it. They were my mother and father and they were lying on a snake. The water came out a spout between my mother's and father's head and they had photographs taken of it.

I do not know how these people met. My mother will tell you a story. In it my mother will be in a nest on a cliff and my father will have climbed the cliff and stole my mother and maybe he will have killed some eggs. My mother came to think the marriage should never have happened even though her childer is made of both the Gillaroo and the Sonaghan. My mother has gone off with Beggy to the London Borough of Enfield and maybe she is telling Beggy stories now about the way Aubrey Sonaghan stole her from her people. Beggy will have to think about who she is and Beggy might think how this marriage came to be. She will think of her sister Margarita and how she got married young and went to live out west and even though Margarita did not marry back into the Gillaroos it was as good because she turned away from the life her father tried to make for her. She will think of me and maybe she will hear that I left the house too, and she will think of Aaron and the things that brought him down. She will think of us scattered and seeded and turned to the soil and maybe she will be right to think this marriage should never have happened.

But it is only a way of looking at it, it does not mean that this is the right way. Even my mother used tell a different story. Even around the time I am thinking, the time her brothers came with Paul, she might have told a different story. The real trouble did not begin until after Aaron killed himself. That as I says was years ahead.

Come close childer my mother says.

We were all of us childer in the one bedroom this night. Beggy got the terrors and she came in the bedroom to me and Aaron because Aaron was the boxer who'd look after her. In came Margarita wondering what all this was about. In came my mother saying there there childer. It is okay you curl up by Aaron's feet she says to Beggy. Margarita and me were sitting on the bed our back on the wall. What is wrong little Kate my mother says stroking the head of Beggy. There there Aaron is here to look after you, Aaron will box them away. See this she says taking down one of Aaron's boxing prizes, this is to ward off the ghosts.

This trophy here she says this is a sign of the strength of your father. Your father put all his anger away to bring two families together.

The Sonaghans and the Gillaroos says Beggy.

Good girl Kate says my mother. The Sonaghans and the Gillaroos it is. And you are very special childer you all are because you are the first childer in hundreds of years who's made of both Sonaghan and Gillaroo. It's been so long that the last childer like that wasn't even people my mother says.

If they wasn't people then what was they mammy says Beggy.

They was fish says my mother. The Sonaghans and the Gillaroos was all once fish. And you heard of this place Melvin where the families is from. All that's there now is a pond but it was all once a lake where the Sonaghan fish and the Gillaroo fish did live. They lived together there and they was happy childer. It was more usual that the Sonaghans would keep to themself and the Gillaroos the same but sometimes a fish from one family would court a fish from the other. A fish from one family if they was trying to court another they would swim around them and the circle would get smaller until both fish was touching. And when two fish like that had babbies then if the father was a Sonaghan then the babby would be a Sonaghan and if the father was a Gillaroo then the babby would be Gillaroo. There was many new Sonaghans and Gillaroos came into the world this way and it was a happy world that lake in Melvin.

But there was a world outside that lake my mother says. Down the length of one shore of it was a farm owned by a fella the name of Dan his name was. The only idea the fish in the lake had of something going on beyond the lake was when Dan's cows would dip their pink nose in the water to have a drink. But other than that they was two separate worlds. This Dan now was a crooked sort. Dan was only the second son of his father and so when his father died the farm should have been passed to the eldest. But you know what Dan did as his father lay dying on his death bed. It was a terrible thing childer, he murdered his older brother.

Did he throw his brother in the lake says Beggy pulling the blanket up toward her mouth afeard and the rest of us laughing at her.

No no Kate he didn't throw his brother in the lake my mother says. So the fish did not know about it. They knew nothing, nothing yet anyhows. We'll say Dan just buried his brother somewhere secret and Dan got the farm and the brother was forgot about. But no one ever gets away with murder childer you know about that. Murder is the blackest sin and leaves a black stain on your soul which is a reminder to the Devil to give you a visit to talk about how you might pay the debt of your terrible sin. And sure enough many years later the Devil did come to Dan. Came to him one dark day Dan was up in a back field by the shore of the lake. He seen this thing the side of his eye burn through the gloom against a blackened bit of wall under the brambles that was hanging down. And in this lonely corner this lonely farm wasn't rightly his own Dan knew he was done for. He knew what all this was about. He hoped what he seen there in front of him might just have been in his head, might just have been the weight of his guilt grown and grown over the years until it became the shape of the Devil, but the Devil let him know it was him in this way. The Devil stuck his hand in Dan's chest like this Anthony look.

My mother pressed her hand up against my heart.

And when he took his hand out of Dan's chest he had a lump of burning coal he was holding there. And that was the sin that Dan been carrying around in him all these years. But that was not the end of it, that was far from the end of it. If Dan thought that the Devil was finished with him he was wrong. The coal was just to show Dan what sin looked like. Dan still had his debt to pay. And when a man has a debt to pay he does not have much power. He is there to be used. The thing about the Devil childer is he is most of all a trickster. If the Devil can get something for himself out of his dealings with men then he will take these opportunities. Nothing is straight and forward. Sometimes he will forget about the debt that has to be paid if he can see a thing to gain. And the Devil saw such an opportunity there in Dan. The Devil asks Dan he says to Dan this.

Do you know of Saint Patrick's Purgatory he says.

Dan said he didn't know of this place. The Devil says to him it is only a day away from Melvin on foot. He says to Dan I will strike a bargain with you. He lifted the lump of coal still burning in his fist to his mouth and blew on it. The flame went out and left in his hand was a small smooth black stone with many glistering tiny blue eyes in it. Then he reached out his hand again and he put the stone back in Dan's chest.

Poor Dan says Beggy.

There wasn't nothing poor about him Kate, there wasn't nothing poor about him. Listen to this. This stone will protect you in what I am about to ask you to do Dan says the Devil.

I want you to travel to Saint Patrick's Purgatory. When you get there I want you to tell the abbot of the monastery that you have been sent to enter the cave behind the altar where you must pay for your sins. Inside the cave you will be attacked by every sort of demon. But the stone now in front of your heart will give you a shield around you that will protect you from any attack. And the stone will light up and show you the way around the miles of tunnels. Let it guide you to the crystal cloisters Dan. There you will find a jewel casket. I want you to take the jewel casket. The stone in your heart will guide you out of the tunnels and back to the mouth of the cave. The abbot will be so shocked to see you again he will drop dead on the spot. Bring the jewels back to me. The Devil says to Dan if you bring me the jewels you might not be free of sin but you will have this I tell you. You will live for ever. God will not be able to touch you because of the stone I have put in your heart. And it is not only this you will enjoy. I will share with you the treasures in the jewel casket Dan. How does that sound to you.

Well Dan was gone before the Devil had even finished talking says my mother. And he got to Saint Patrick's Purgatory a lot quicker than the day the Devil said it would take because he ran the whole way the thoughts of the jewels and of all the time he would have to be spending his wealth now in his head. Down in the tunnels the stone in Dan's chest guided Dan just as the Devil told him it would, the blue eyes in it throwing a weird light about. And any demon that threw themself at Dan crashed and broke against him like an egg falling on the ground from a height. And the jewels was there exactly as the Devil said they would be, in the crystal cloisters.

And the abbot got such a fright seeing Dan come back out the cave and appear behind the altar he fell over dead. And Dan was back home at the farm in Melvin on the shore the lake even quicker than the time it took him going the other way because he was anxious to see this deal done with the Devil.

Dan was there waiting by the bit of blackened wall in the back field by the shore the last place he seen the Devil anyhows childer my mother says. He could hear the water splashing gentle and the odd cow mooing and he says hear me Devil wherever you are I am back from my adventure and I have the jewel casket for you. And he seen the air change in front of him, he seen the Devil start to appear and the first part of the Devil he seen appear was the eyes. The Devil's eyes was huge and green and fastened on them jewels with Dan. The next part of him to appear was his arms and his arms was swaying sort of, they was not quite joined at the hands but they was swaying like this childer, like they was rocking a babba. Dan now this point was feeling afeard, it did not feel right, but he swallowed hard anyhows and he says to the Devil's eyes here is the jewel casket you asked for Devil. Why don't we open it here and see what we have and divide up the jewels like you said Devil master he says. But this is what happened childer. The Devil's arms that was swaying shot out all a sudden and they grabbed the jewel casket from Dan's arms. The arms and the jewels disappeared into the air. Then the eyes turned up to face Dan and they went narrow and they was gone too.

Devil Devil where are you screamed Dan. Devil Devil you tricked me he says after realising the Devil was not coming back. Devil what about our bargain he shouting louder than he shouted in his life. What about our bargain he says now whining. He fell to his knees, he was depressed was the only way. But then he remembered the stone the Devil had left in his chest. The Devil being so quick to get away with the jewels forgot to take the stone back out of Dan and it lifted Dan to think that he had that, that he would live for ever. He thought he would test it to see was it true, to see would the stone protect him from dying just like it had when he was in the cave with the demons. So he took a length of bramble from the brambles creeping over the wall and he tied it in a noose. He climbed up with the twists of a buckled grey tree and he tied one end of the bramble to the tree and he put the noose around his neck. And he says here I go he says to himself and he jumped off toward the ground. But childer childer. He did not know one thing. He did not know that death by his own hand was the only death could get to him, that the stone would not protect him from. Because childer when a man kills himself it is the Devil's work, it is the Devil doing the killing. And the Devil knew the stone in front of Dan's heart, he knew to get around it. And Dan hung there from the tree and he had neither jewels now nor life. He hung there dead.

All this time the noise Dan been making made other people notice including God. His shouting had gone out across the water and all around the hills. It went to the nearest town and the town nearest that. It travelled right over the county and into the counties either side. It hit off every wall and it echoed up to Heaven. And do you think God was happy with Dan childer. Anthony do you think God was happy with Dan.

I think God was not happy with Dan I says.

God was not happy with Dan my mother says. What's this about bargains with the Devil his voice comes booming. What is all this. And God looked down where the shouts was coming and he seen Dan there hanging and he knows Dan done the two worst things a man could do, he done a deal with the Devil and he killed himself. Well three things because he murdered his brother too. God was so angry he wanted to do something to Dan right that minute but he could not because Dan was dead. It is not often God gets in a blind rage but this is just what happened him with this greedy murdering sinning farmer. He looked about for ways to take his anger out on Dan, any way at all. The Blessed Mother was one side of him on her knees shaking violent saying please show mercy Lord but nothing could calm God. He looked about and then he seen Dan's cows by the lake. So this is what he done childer. He seen Dan's cows and he says I will make them cows suffer. They will feel the full power of my anger. He seen some of them was supping from the lake and he spun his hand and the water in the lake lowered and lowered. It went right down until the cows was staring at a puddle. And then the puddle disappeared through the mud in the bottom and the lake was gone and the cows was just as good as finished childer. But can you think what else was after happening.

The fish says Aaron.

The Sonaghans, the Gillaroos says Beggy.

This is it now. The Gillaroos there and the Sonaghans, the poor fish suffering from the greed the evils this farmer Dan. They was left there the bottom the lake no water, the thing it was they needed to survive. God was in no mood to help fishes this point and he went off to lie down so angry was he still with Dan. But the Blessed Mother was still looking down off the edge of Heaven. She seen the fishes on the bottom what used to be the lake and they was rolling about and they was suffocating childer because they needed the water to breathe. What are we to do about these poor creatures the Blessed Mother said to herself. She said whatever is needed for these fishes to survive let it happen because it is not their doing the sins of this crooked farmer. And she closed her eyes and she thought very hard and soon the fishes felt the power of her thoughts. It started as a warmth childer, they did no longer feel the cold air around them. Their bodies was changing see, changing from the inside. Soon it was that the air was natural for them. They found themself breathing the air the next thing. They took a breath and they thought there would be no hope because there was no water but then it was that the air came in their nose and filled their body and their body grew bigger. The scales came off them then and underneath was skin, human skin childer. They seen that their fins turned to arms and legs and their head came forward and hair grew out the top. Then one of them took it on him to stand up use his new legs. The others seen him and the rest them stood up too. And all them was standing there now the bottom this lake looking at each other wondering what's gone on. They was people now. That was the moment the Gillaroos and the Sonaghans became people childer.

God now this time had had his lie down and was wondering what the Blessed Mother was doing still the edge of Heaven. He went back where they been earlier and there he seen her looking down on what she was after creating. Then it came back to him what he done himself, the anger that filled him over Dan. He says I am down on people Mother. But I am too tired to do much about it. It would take an effort to finish all these people off. So I am going to curse them and let them finish each other off instead what he says.

The next thing the Gillaroos and the Sonaghans were looking at one another suspicious. They could not work it out what it was they even was yet but each one knew inside themself which person came from which family. And each member of each family looked at the members the other family with something near hatred now. It came through in them this way. All they knew was that this pit in the ground they was standing in was home but because they was people there was not much room left and all of them crowded in the one space. So each family knew they would have to get rid of the other family to make the space for their own. And it was a Sonaghan struck out first. I am not saying nothing childer but it was a member the Sonaghans swung first. But if he didn't then a Gillaroo would have. By the end that day the whole of what used be the bottom the lake in Melvin was full of fighting, the men facing up to one another in the middle and the women stood against the banks at the back. By the next morning one of the families I don't know which made a break through the others and they went straight for the women of the other family. The women was so in fear of their life they climbed up the bank in a panic. And now it was they was out in the wider world childer. There could be enough space for the both families if they could see it.

But they could not. God's curse because of the sins of a farmer was still on them. There was blood in their nostrils and hate in their heart. They could not stop fighting now. The families chased one another over the fields one way and back ten times the distance the other way. The fighting spread from field to field to farm to farm, from county to county and then from one age to another. It kept going childer, the curse, the fighting. This awful tormenting power driving both families.

My mother stopped talking. She stroked Beggy's head again and took Aaron's boxing prize.

But don't you worry Kate my chicken says my mother. This story has a happy ending. And that because of your father. Your father who was the greatest fighter there ever was, who took on all them not just the Gillaroos. It was looking like he could have finished off the Gillaroos he wanted to. There wasn't no one could beat him and there was plenty tried be the king of the country let me tell you. Plenty looked at your father thought they could be like him. That was the sort of man your father is. He is a giant and a hero childer. What he does others do too. So he got to the point he knew he had the power to do anything. He could continue on the road he was on or he could make the peace. And you know that is what he done. And the first people he went to make the peace with was the Gillaroos. It was like the curse was broken.

Is the curse broken says Beggy.

Course the curse is broken my child says my mother. The families won't go back to those ways no more. If they want to fight they do what Aaron does and win prizes for it.

And now childer my mother says you must turn in for the night. That is enough of the stories and I hope you sleep better now Kate.

The next morning my father was angry with my mother. I seen it myself. My mother said she went in to him after talking to us childer and she had to turn off the radio he after falling asleep the radio on. My father says was that so, was that so. He tore at the very buttered bread with his teeth.

I don't want you telling them childer no stories he says to my mother.

How could you hear me telling them stories you sitting up with the radio on she says. You don't even know what I was saying. I was talking good things about you. I was telling them happy stories.

He says I knew by the sound of your voice you were telling them stories. I could hear it through the wall. I don't want no stories in this house no more. They want stories they can read books he says.

The next years then were bad. My mother left with Beggy and most the things in the house she used to want she left behind. She did not want them any more and now there was no one to clean them. My father was bent over in this mess and the things were getting dirty.

8

There were days them weeks with Arthur in that room that house I would think well of him and there were days I was angry the trials could have come down on me.

All I knew them first early days was this was the rest of my life. I seen it ahead of me, I seen it staring back at me. The two of us looking one another cross a room, the two of us watching television in the blue in the evening, in the gloom, a man saying the world would end, ice sliding into the sea, bad news. Years it would be. Every day, Lynx stinging my eye, every Thursday morning, this game, get out of here now before the landlord comes, I am not going nowhere he says. Friday, in the landing, in the shower singing oh solo holy lowly me oh. I would see marks of his feet on the carpet on the stair I says that is him, these marks will go black.

I would let him go off in the streets on his own. First time I says to him you don't know those streets, he says I will find my way. First time he went he got lost, he could not find the Spar, he came straight back. I says help me, help me someone, that is what you do. I went to the Spar myself I thinks I will keep going, I will leave him in that room. Sometimes I got angry, I will abandon him I says. But sometimes we would walk the streets together, we would not say a word about troubles, walking the streets was all that we needed. We would look above at windows and see the skill of the iron worker. We would see the great barrel shafts down the back of our houses. We would walk to the maternity hospital we would see the sheep's skulls under the eaves. We tried the sample preserved lemons in a shop for Arabs, they would make you cough and cry. We watched drunk Polish men fish the water of the old canal basin beneath the skin of oil and feathers. We watched them sway and we laughed, we watched them get caught we laughed louder. Arthur said the next warm day that came he would swim to the island in the middle, he didn't care what no sign said. One morning we were at peace on a street on a hill. There was a fog after falling on the city but the sun was burning through, it was not a bright sun and it was pure white. We stood on a corner looking down the street, we looked at the buildings. One evening we got in a hall. We looked at the ceiling made us admire our Celtic past. We stood with our hands behind our back. It was easy to think of the richness in the world. Moments like this I would not think of the danger might have come down on us. Came to a point I had let the fear go, I felt secure was the way.

One evening my fear came back to me. This evening Arthur went out to get drink. After an hour he was not back. I panicked I could not stop it. I says to myself I will need to get tablets with this. My hands shook, they were sweating, the lines on them were clear and glistering, the lines opened out, they were like cuts, I could not read these lines. If I believed in these things if I could read these things I would have seen my days ahead were not good and they were not mine to do anything with.

And strange but before he even tapped the button I had the feel he was back at the front door. But there was nothing strange about it, was his voice only distant what it was and he gone and tapped the wrong button what he done.

This damn key you gave me isn't worth nothing can't get it to turn in the lock he screams up from the street.

Easy easy I says and I had the window slid up and I was at him to shush. Will you whisht I says and I'll be down a minute.

I seen him disappear under the doorway, the door after opening below, and I waited there the second. No one came out on the steps and fuck him I says. Sure enough on the stair I passed one of the African fellas bounding up and Arthur in the hall below the gawp on him taking in the surrounds like this was the first he seen them.

You okay I says to him. Up close I seen he was sweating too.

Fine he says, look at this.

He had my bag on him. He turned around I seen it was full of tins.

Twelve tins ten euros he says.

I says to him you're sweating like you were running.

He says I wasn't running, think I can run with me foot the way it is.

There isn't nothing wrong with your foot no more I says.

I'm crippled he says.

I says you're no cripple you're a torment to me.

He says but that's a fine window you have over the door with the purple and the gold in it and you only see the effect this side of it.

I waved him forward to the stair I says watch it now get up and keep your eyes off that lead.

It's lead in the window is it he says.

I says get up now and mind the bit of carpet.

What countries do these fellas be coming from he says.

I says will you get up and stop this, this.

In the room I'd made food for the both of us. The food had gone cold, I had to heat it again, but stirring the pot was good for settling the worries. There been a thing on the television about another son of Martin Thresh Sonaghan Lee the name of Showbiz Joseph Thresh. Showbiz had went after the boys had killed his brother Damien Thresh three month back. He went looking through Limerick was the story, been told the murderers were there. But he had to do it quiet and he was so quiet he didn't hear nothing. He left and went home to Galway. A few nights later he went out of a pub between Galway and Tuam. The people in the pub heard a bang and they went out and Showbiz was dead on the ground shot in the side of the head.

Arthur was looking through books been on my floor these last six month. They were given to me by Judith but I didn't know if she wanted them back. He lifted the one at the top of the pile like he was looking for a louse under a stone. He opened it and closed it.

He says to me do you know your father is learning to read.

I says no I did not.

He's getting lessons says Arthur. He's with this new church and he's getting lessons off them. And he told me he's getting good at it.

I poured out the dinner I says that fucking church is filling his head all kinds of shit.

Arthur says let me show you something.

He went over to his camp bed and he got out from under it the white sack I found him with at the Spar that first day. He took out a magazine, threw it down in front of me.

He sends away for that, gives them money says Arthur. He gave it me in the hospital but there's parts of it he can't understand.

The magazine was four pages big. The front page was filled with words except for a picture of a man with no hair and black glasses. I could not read the words myself, they were in another language. The words across the top of the page said Iglesia Católica de Utrera.

Me father is a holy man do you think I says.

He is big into the prayer, the power of prayer says Arthur.

Is that what he tells you I says.

A change has come on him Anthony says Arthur.

What sort of change I says.

He feels a peace says Arthur. He tells me he seen it, he seen the way, that he knows what to do with his life. He told me it's like, and Arthur stopped.

I says go on so what he say this brother of yours that's good with the words.

Arthur says he says it's like he's taken a cold strong beer and he felt the chills inside him but calm the first instant. It's a feeling he hasn't been able to get rid of he told me.

That so I says. I looked at the picture of the man on the magazine. He was foreign, he was Spanish, it was Pope David of Utrera. A holy man I says again.

He talks to the saints says Arthur. Saint Eoin O'Duffy is his big thing now, he tells me he has a picture of him on his wall.

Does he ask Saint Eoin O'Duffy for help I says.

He does says Arthur.

Is Saint Eoin O'Duffy there to help I says.

I don't know says Arthur.

Or does he chastise like God I says.

That is something I do not know says Arthur. All you can do is ask.

Do you think me father is a holy man I says.

I do says Arthur. I do he says and he got up off the couch and went over to the bin and started rooting in it. He took out an empty tin of Club, put it sitting up on the floor. He put his bad foot on it and lifted the other so as the tin got crushed.

I says there's no bother with the foot now I see.

He says we will get another bag for the tins and that. We will have a bag for the recycling. See them rolls of green bags left in the hall he says. They're for the recycling, we should take a few of them and find out when the men come around and collect them.

I says me father is a shamed person and he is sick in the head.

And this he says, he was not listening. He took the box for the tea bags out the bin. That's cardboard he says.

I says do you hear me.

He came back over and sat on the couch. He took a tin of beer and opened it, then he reached in his trousers and took out a new packet of cigarettes. He said to me did I want one.

You know I don't fucking smoke no more I says. He lit up and I says I have decided I don't want smoking in this room. And the landlord will kick you out for doing it I says.

He paid no heed to me.

I says do you hear me.

His head went dark as the tip of his cigarette went red.

He says there was reasons your father was bad to your mother.

You don't know about no reasons I says.

I know enough says Arthur. Your mother could be antagonising.

He took the cigarette from his lips. He kept looking at me expecting me to jump back at him but I didn't so he said it again.

Your mother could be antagonising he says. You will agree.

I am letting you go on I says.

He finished the whole of his cigarette then he spoke again. But he says. There isn't no point beating on about them Gillaroos.

Well be quiet about them I says.

There isn't no point to the feuding only causes grief he says.

You should hear you I says.

And look at what I'm saying he says.

I am I says. I am thinking of the time of Aaron's burial and what you said and did then. I am thinking of you throwing stones at helicopters. You did not look like a man wanting to bury a feud I says.

It was nothing he says. A bit of messing.

I am thinking of all your words about them I says.

He laughed then he went serious. I'll tell you Anthony that was the moment for me he says.

Which now I says.

He would not answer.

Hello I says, are you gone deaf.

Your brother's burial he says. That was the time I decided he says.

What did you decide I says.

That I wanted no more of the old life he says.

Yes I says. And then you hit the road again for three year like the best of them.

He lit another cigarette, but it was not to chastise, I could see, and I did not say anything.

That was for no love of the road he says.

That night Arthur was restless. I had my eyes closed and I was tired but I could hear the wires in the camp bed creaking, I could hear the click of his lighter. One stage he moved to the window to smoke. I did not tell him to stop, I did not say anything. I was tired, I was thinking about my father. I was thinking about what Arthur had said about him. Me father now the reader I thinks. The reader now, wha. Well what brought that on I thinks. A change had come over him said Arthur. Oh, a change. I seen a change come on him all right. His hands into fists, the blood to his head. A change, and when it came it came quick.

When I went asleep I seen again my father hitting my mother. There was music following every swing of the arm. The picture of that was in my head, the sound of it. It was slower than real and he was beating but there was a skill or a grace to his moving. When I woke out of it the music was still going in my head, it was the classical music. There was also in my head a question. The question was repeating. You learnt to read now father was the question. It was a question but I couldn't get at the first word of it, the where or the how or the why. Or maybe I was just saying it to myself, like it was inevitable.

I thought Arthur was still awake, I says out loud where did this thing the Sonaghan side of me family come that we want to be improving ourself the whole time.

There was no answer from him.

I says did it come from me grandfather.

He did not answer this question neither and I thought he was asleep then but I woke the next morning with the sound of him coming in the door of the room. He been out most the night walking it turned out.

I took your key this time he says.

I says you okay.

He says I'm tired of the walking, and he fell on the couch and slept.

9

The Cliffs were the houses Arthur and my father lived in when they were young men. Hundreds of years before in this place they blew out the stones that built the city and the name the Cliffs came because one side was a cliff. Before they built the houses the Cliffs was only a camp where my grandfather and grandmother and my father as a young fella and Arthur as a baba lived for some of the year. Some men came down from Dublin one time asked for cannon balls and the men of the camp went in their wagons and got the men from Dublin cannon balls weighing in their hand. It got the men from Dublin's interest and the next there was a gang of these fellas came down raked the land and cleared the site and got more cannon balls from the time of Wolfe Tone. Soon after this the houses were built.

In the Cliffs the people grew vegetables. The soil was rich but it wasn't only the soil made the vegetables grow, it was that the Cliffs was down in the ground. One side of the Cliffs was the high wall of stone, the other side the other way was open to the fields, but the side the wall of stone was was the side the wind blew in. It blew over the tops of the houses and the vegetables were protected. My father said he seen it from a young age, seen the people in the Cliffs build glass houses, they built a town of them, built tunnels of them, the glass houses ran one into the next. The frames of them were made of wood treated with gum and of metal they beat into shapes that were needed, metal from farms and from houses that came down. In the frames they put the glass and they put sheets sacks and blankets.

But the man with the Perspex came. He was not a strange man the people thought. Arthur thought that he wore blue. The man done them all a deal. The glass came out and the Perspex was put in. In two year the Perspex had lines across it and the dirt set in the lines and the Perspex turned yellow. Someone had the idea to lift up part of the Perspex because it closed all the gaps. He said the old glass and sheets sacks and blankets did not close all the gaps and the vegetables needed to breathe the air. They lifted part of the Perspex but it did not help the vegetables, they would not grow any more. Some people were defeated by it.

But that is the story of the Cliffs.

My father met my mother when he was twenty three or twenty four or twenty five and he left the Cliffs when they got married. Arthur lived in the Cliffs until he was thirty four and he got hassle because he just could not find the right woman. Some people thought he was queer. He was not queer, he liked young girls.

Arthur met Teresa Gillaroo when he was thirty two and he brought her to live in the Cliffs when he was thirty three. I know it about the age of them because she was sixteen and Arthur was twice the girl's age when they met, I know because it was talked about at the time.

Arthur was crazy about this girl. I am saying that. He learnt about her in our house. He would come to our house. My mother liked him. He would let on he did not need my mother to look after him. Of all the Sonaghans my mother should have married Arthur and I am not joking. Arthur would say me brother got himself a Gillaroo where is there one for me and my mother would hit him on the head and say you will get your chance don't be impatient and Arthur would say the families will fall out again by then.

This time Arthur and my father and Aaron and me were talking in our house and my mother was speaking on the phone with one of her cousins in Rath. The cousin told her another one of their cousins was running in a race in Dublin. My mother did not say to us about her cousin in the race because she did not care. Then late in the evening she said it about her. My father said what cousin. Teresa my mother says.

She is a little bitch you do not know she says. My father asked my mother where the race was on. She said she did not know. It's in the Phoenix Park then she says. Sure we'll go my father says. He was interested by the people got involved in sports because Aaron got taken in by the boxing club.

They went to the race but I did not go. My father took my mother and Arthur. I heard of some of it later. I seen Teresa a year after and the picture I have in my head of her in the park was she was thin. Somebody had seen her running about Rath and they said she should join the club for the runners. They seen she had the body for it. Her legs were like the front of knives. Arthur was looking at her body and he wanted her body. Arthur and my mother and father were on a hill and watched her come around on the grass and when the runners disappeared behind the trees Arthur went running through the trees. He skidded down the other side of the hill in the trees and the birds flew everywhere and the deers stood up. When he came out the other side of the trees he had to dig his heel in the ground to stop himself and his head stopped just in time. The runners went past him a minute after and he was getting his breath.

He drove down to Rath. He knew he was taking a risk and he drove around Rath instead of into Rath. He went in a pub in another town. The bar man was going to kick him out but then Arthur damned the people in Rath. He got to talking about sports and Arthur is a friendly man. He asked the man about running. The man said there was a running club not too far and he told Arthur where it was.

The running club had the times for the training outside of it and Arthur can read numbers. He waited outside two times in a row and then Teresa came along. He did not want her body this moment, it was not this simple. He just wanted to go with her now because he loved this girl because he felt he was looking after her by driving across Ireland for her. But he did not know what to say to her. He said to her he was the brother in law of her cousin Kate Gillaroo now Kate Sonaghan up in Dublin. Then he thought of this. He said to her that the walk back to Rath was a long way and she after been running. He gave her a lift toward Rath but he stopped outside the town. He was straight up with her. He says if I go in there it will not be good.

Arthur drove two evenings every week over a hundred mile to this same spot outside Rath. He met Teresa there and he would take her to the running club. She was glad of the lift to the running club because in the evenings she was worn out and she was glad of the lift back because the running made her more worn out. Arthur said she would run better because she wouldn't be tired. Teresa thought of this and one day when she got in the van she said she loved Arthur. They kissed like the cowboy and his girl.

Because Arthur was in love with Teresa he wanted her to do well with the running but he knew he could not go in the running club. Every evening when Teresa was doing the training Arthur would drive around, maybe he would go fishing in the moon or sit eating in Yankee Doodles. He would think in these hours and he thought he would train her himself. He went in a shop in Dublin and he got talking to the fella. The fella sold him a stop clock and showed him how to use it. He went around with a stop clock and a rain coat for a year and the people in the Cliffs laughed behind his back. Then they seen Teresa had moved in the Cliffs with him and they did not know if they should laugh.

In the mornings Arthur stood in the field near the Cliffs and he pressed his stop clock and Teresa would run away from him and across the new motor way being built and into the bottom of the hills and she would come back. They never left one another's sight all this time now. When they were not doing the running Teresa was at home in the Cliffs with Arthur or she was with him in the van when he was travelling selling bowls and three legged tables. They were never separated but Teresa's father would not allow them marry even when Arthur rang him. Arthur told Teresa this. He said too that her father said he didn't want Teresa in the family no more. Arthur and Teresa kissed again like cowboys.

Some time after Teresa was not happy. Arthur seen that Teresa was getting depressed and he thought it might have been because she was separated from her family in Rath. He thought that she did not know this herself and he did not want to say it for her. He says I want to make you happy girl what is the matter. Teresa said to Arthur she had not run in a race a long time and it was making her low. She also said about the time she was in Dublin the time of the race in the Phoenix Park. She said that after the race all the girls in the running club were taken into Dublin and they went to McDonald's and drank strawberry milk shakes. Teresa said to Arthur that when she came up to Dublin with Arthur she thought she would drink strawberry milk shakes in McDonald's every night, that she was dreaming about it every night. Arthur says well that is it, we will go to McDonald's every night and drink strawberry milk shakes.

A few month before Teresa went off on Arthur two things happened. One was that Teresa got too fat to run. The other thing that happened was that one day when Arthur and Teresa came back from a day working in the van some of the others in the Cliffs came up to them and they were agitated. They said that when Arthur and Teresa were away some fellas they did not like the look of came asking after the two of them. They had banged on Arthur's door and they shouted through the letter box. They took a look around the side of the house but one of the neighbours came out and said words with them. The neighbour that did this said to Arthur that the fellas were not raring, but funny about it that was what no one liked about them. The fellas had asked when Arthur and Teresa would be back but the neighbour told them to fuck off and the fellas went away laughing.

Arthur says to Teresa I won't let you out of my sight baby baby I won't. He says we must never leave you alone. He said he would show her everything there was to do with numbers, that she could do the work the same as he did. He said they would go on holidays over in other countries. He says to hell with it I will marry you I don't care what your father thinks.

This did not happen the way Arthur wanted. Teresa would not think about dresses, she would not look at rings. She got more depressed but Arthur would hold her by the cheek and kiss her on the head and she would smile. Even though she was fat Arthur said he loved her more than ever, she was his baby. He was with her longer than any other girl and she gave him something different to do. She gave him a great laugh and she said it herself then that she loved him more than anyone and that it didn't matter what her family thought she would stay with him, and in the dark he said they would have their own babbies.

But one time Arthur turned into the Cliffs and there was smoke coming from the house. The people were around the front of the house and they ran to Arthur when he came up to the house. He jumped out the van and he was crying. He was shouting Teresa Teresa. He ran to get in the house and one of the neighbours took Arthur by the arm. He said Teresa was fine. Arthur says where is she. The man said Teresa was fine. Arthur says I need to see her. The man said he couldn't see her. Arthur says I thought you said she was fine. The man said she was fine. Arthur says how do you know she's fine. The man said she was fine because there was no sign of her when the fire brigade put out the fire. He said she'd left by the time the fire was lit.

A late wet sunny May evening Arthur came to our house smelling of smoke. He puked on our table. He was gone on the boat in July.

10

The longer myself and Arthur went on, the two of us in this damp broken room, the more I thought about getting back in with Judith. I wanted to kill the guilt because the guilt was getting at me for letting her down, I am an awful guilty man sometimes. I wanted to get back a good thing, I wanted to get out the house this situation and have something to do was the truth. I wanted to bring her back her books. I don't know. But I could not think of how to get back with her.

One of the days I says to Arthur you think you could get to liking these streets.

I could and I am liking them he says.

And this I says. This whole life I says.

What about it he says.

You think you could get to liking it too I says. This settled life.

Sure isn't it the life that is natural for me he says.

I laughed loud. You're serious I says.

Didn't I grow up in a house he says.

You grew up in a house surrounded by the rest of them I says. Other houses like it and the same people all around.

Sure what do you know what's settled he says.

I'm not saying I know anything I says.

There you are he says.

No I know one thing I says.

What is it he says.

Most the people in this country are wrong in their ways I says. Any old person you see, any young person you see, anything they say, anything they have and anything they hold to is wrong.

What's that he says.

Something I got off that woman Judith I told you about I says.

We should go to her he says.

Yes I says.

Serious he says.

I'm not going nowhere with you I says.

Why he says.

I'm shamed of you I says.

That's harsh words now he says. Why you shamed of me.

Haven't you been living in a van these last years I says.

No I have not he says.

Where did you sleep your nights on the road then I says.

I slept in guesthouses he says.

Guesthouses I says.

And people's homes he says. People invited me in.

Where I says.

In France, in England, all over he says. They call me a man of the world is the thing they say about me. They invite me in.

Like some tinker, depending on the hospitality of others I says.

I wasn't depending on no one he says.

And whatever happened that van I says.

I sold it he says. I'm thinking about buying something smaller.

Like a car I says.

Yes he says. Something that suits me needs. I'm keeping an eye out around me.

What are your needs I says.

I'll tell you he says.

Tell me I says.

Hospitality he says. That's a big word. What does it mean.

You know what it fucking means I says. Are you thick I says.

Could be he says.

So you want hospitality I says. Living off the hospitality of me here because you're tired of life on the road.

That's not it he says. Although for a while it would, what do the people say, it would be nice.

You can fuck off with your nice I says.

Just to get established like he says.

Until I says.

Until he says. Well he says. What is until.

Until is the time you get out of here I says.

No he says. Until is the time before then.

I can tell you it won't be a long time I says. How long are you planning it to be.

How long does it take to learn he says.

Learn what I says.

The words he says.

What words I says.

Big words he says. Like hospitality. He says I'll tell you in plain simple words. I want to be seeing what's in books, I want to learn to read and to write he says.

Yes you do I says.

Serious he says. I want to learn to read and to write.

Who's going to teach you that I says.

I think I got it in meself he says. Sure don't we know it's in the family with you and your father. I just need the little assistance see. I need the bit of help with it he says.

He got up from the couch, went over to the gas rings, over to the window. Moving, going nowhere, not looking at me. He was like my father when he moved. This wide back on him. The way he walked too, lifting and falling, showing he was a heavy crooked man. The limp in his foot made it worse.

Sometimes I was shamed of this person it was true but maybe I should not been shamed. I seen another thing with him now the way the light caught him from the side. It was the mouth on him, the lines that led to his lips. I stroked my own face thinking did I have them lines myself but I don't think I have them.

I says to him do you know.

He held the end of the bed, he turned to me, he says what.

Storytelling man let me tell you something I says.

What he says.

This lady Judith would like to meet you I am sure I says.

I went for a walk down to the university the next day not thinking. I was mooching, the beautiful young ones going by, I says no I will leave. Then I seen this thing. Words on sheets of paper on a wall and I read them, was stopped by them, there was hundreds of them, I read them quick.

They said Freshers Week Table Quiz in aid of Jurgen Clemente at the Phil on why Revive A new approach to worship Love God Embrace God Be Challenged By God Nuzum Hall off White boy soul night featuring Legs Akimbo White Chocolate and Ladyshave Whitebrassgate Theatre Group is holding auditions Wednesday noon for The Cherry Orchard A Play by Anton Chekhov House 6.

Whitebrassgate was the name of the group Judith had set up and today was a Monday, two days the auditions it said.

The Wednesday then myself and Arthur walked to the university together. A bright day, a good day for a start. The city looked different because we were in a certain mood, I imagined it. We walked past the steps of the cathedral where there was a market in the gates where the ladies were selling their cakes. I went up the steps after Arthur and he bought a bag of them. He says I know that other lady I've sold her videos and he says thank you missus did you make these yourself. We leaned on the wall to eat the cakes. The lady shouts mind your teeth because there were decorations on the cakes. Across the street I pointed to Arthur the chipper where I bought chips once and the junkies that were hanging about. I said they would not give us trouble but we moved on.

We got to the river and he says it is a fine place. The water was down, it was something I seen before. The sea weed was on the walls of the river and the air smelt of salt, you would breathe it in.

He says how many bridges is there on the river.

I says I don't know, about ten.

He says the last bridge is a toll bridge, and he pointing over toward where the sea was. He says that was the way I came into Dublin before. Do you remember some of the times. You used come with me.

I only remember the one time I says. I says do you like this part of Dublin.

I do he says.

I says wait until you look at the university, and we went over the river.

The university was different all these last few days. There were great things going on this week. We went in under the arch and both sides were tables and stalls set out said Historical Society and Science Fiction Society and Players. There were flags and balloons, a girl throwing sweets from a bucket.

There were girls everywhere with big T shirts pulled over their clothes. The first thing Arthur says was he liked the girls. I says you haven't seen nothing like these girls before. He nodded at one with red hair wheeling a bicycle. We watched her jump on the saddle and move off in the dark under the arch to the street. Arthur sat down behind the stalls on a black heavy chain swung between posts.

I says wait there.

I went in the shop and I bought two golden delicious.

I says to him these are the cheapest in Dublin.

He says this is something else this chain the work went into it, he was only interested in the chain now.

I says come on we'll look at the rest of the university.

We walked to the tennis courts where there was a beautiful surface. They were surrounded all sides by buildings and the noise of the ball echoed around and the girls' breaths was steaming in the cold air. We came out by the grandest building in the university. It looked like a tomb because everything about it was pointed to the sky. It was built for the students were killed fighting in the first war was what I'd learnt. The oldest tree that was in Ireland was on the lawn across from the building and facing the lawn was the red brick building that was the oldest in the university and the library that was the biggest in the world one point.

These are the oldest and biggest buildings in Ireland I says to Arthur.

Behind the red brick building was the library where Judith worked and the museum they kept the bones of dead animals and the field a game of rugby was going on. The grass in the field was in a bad way, it was cut up from rain early in the day.

We watched the rugby game ten minutes, we watched them running into sacks of sand.

Arthur says it's a good game, it's a carrying game he says.

I says what does that mean.

He says they have to carry the ball.

I says I like it when they kick the ball, you can hear it and feel it in your chest.

He says it'd make you want to join in it would.

I says to him do you think you could run on that foot now.

He says I probably could but I won't today.

We went to move and turned around and we came facing this fella coming down the path. He was a student and he seen Arthur was smoking. He stopped and he says to Arthur have you got a light.

I do young man says Arthur.

The fella put his cigarette in his mouth and Arthur lifted his lighter. The breeze was coming in from the side.

Move around this way says Arthur.

The fella was a few year younger than me but he was baldy and he had a moustache that came around to meet the bit of his hair that was over his ears.

When the cigarette was lit Arthur says to him do you take drugs.

No says the fella.

Do you not says Arthur.

I'm not interested says the fella.

Neither am I says Arthur.

I'm a Christian says the fella.

Good man says Arthur. So am I he says.

Are you enjoying freshers week says the fella.

I am says Arthur.

Would you be interested in attending a church meeting says the fella.

I might be says Arthur.

The fella was holding sheets of paper and he gave Arthur one of them. Arthur looked at the paper and said thank you.

When the fella walked on Arthur shouted behind him good man. Good man he shouted again and again and it sounded over the field. The two of us were holding ourself in we were laughing so much.

I can read one word on this and it's God Arthur says looking at the bit of paper.

Very good I says.

Will we give it your father he says.

He has enough with God I says.

We looked out over the field, the fellas playing the rugby on the left, the young people standing eating burgers on the right. I got a sudden and strange and windy feeling like I was intruding. It was a feeling was gone again but it was a true feeling.

Will we go and meet this woman he says.

We will I says.

Where will we go he says.

She works in the library I says, and I turned around showed him the building.

Doesn't look like a library he says.

What's a library meant to look like I says.

Smaller he says. Like the back of a truck he says.

This is a different sort of library I says.

It's big, it's brutal he says.

It's meant to be a safe place I says.

Will we go in he says.

I'll go in I says.

Will I go in he says.

You don't have the card to get in I says.

Where do you get the card he says.

I got it from her I says.

Will you get her to get me a card he says.

I'll see about it I says.

We got to the front of the library and I says to Arthur wait here but I went to the door and I stopped.

He says what's the bother.

I says what am I doing.

You're going to go up there to her room he says.

And what'll I say I says.

And you'll bring her down here to me he says.

I can't be doing this I says.

Why can't you he says.

It's begging I says.

It's not begging how's it begging he says.

It's stupid I says.

Come on now we've walked this far he says.

It's turning up at her door I says.

Isn't that how you used to meet her he says.

No I says. She gave me the card for getting in for to read books not to be banging on her door I says.

How did you be calling on her so he says.

I went to the lady at the desk and said I'm here to see Judith I says.

Do that Arthur says.

Let me think I says.

What's the bother with you he says.

She said goodbye the last time I'm not doing this I says.

What he says.

When I was with her the last time in the canteen she said to me goodbye I says.

Goodbye like fuck off he says.

Yes I says. I can't be going to the desk and asking for her I says.

Do it he says.

I'm not going in announcing I says.

You're weak he says.

We'll think I says.

The fucking midges this place he says.

What I says.

He smacked his cheek, he threw his hand in the air, he walked on down the steps.

Come here I says, but he would not stop. I did not like the way he was dressed. He had on him his old jumper and his hair was a state, it had jam in it.

Come here I says, I caught up with him. I says there's another thing we could do. There's another thing we could do and it is this. I told him about these auditions, that we might meet Judith there.

A while later we found the place the auditions for the play called The Cherry Orchard was on, by the arch. I said we would only have a look and see what they were doing. A sign with an arrow said auditions second floor. We went up to the room. The wall outside it was matt and gloss. Arthur touched the wall and moved a lump of paint around with his finger.

I says leave it.

Arthur says I know the words that's stuck up there they say wet paint.

I says we're not here for those words we're here for these words.

There was a table set up with a box on it. The box was open and in it were sheets of paper. A girl came and she took some of the sheets.

Is that the play you're taking says Arthur to the girl.

Yeah she says.

She went to go down the stair.

Where you going I says to her. The auditions is on in the room I says.

The auditions aren't on for another three quarters of an hour the girl says. I'm taking the script for the read through she says.

Arthur says the read through, and he took one of the plays.

Thank you missus I says to the girl. I turned to Arthur I says what you going to do with that.

We'll have a read through he says.

Come on and we'll get a cup of tea and a burger I says.

We went to the canteen and we had the two cakes we had left and two cups of tea and two burgers. I put the play out on the table.

You smooth it like this Arthur says. He hit it and moved his hand up it. You know I done plays meself times gone back he says.

No I didn't I says.

I got mixed up with this crowd that drove the cinema mobile that put on the plays at the side of the church he says.

I was Moses in a play I enjoyed it I did. Now you has jazz he says.

I says what's that.

That's a line from a play he says.

I read the front of the play, it said The Cherry Orchard by Anton Chekhov adapted by Judith Neill.

Arthur says what's it about.

I says I don't know give us the time to read it here. The first words is Ireland, the late nineteenth century.

A long time ago Arthur says.

It is I says.

Is the next words a long time ago he says.

No I says.

Read me some words of it and I'll show you the way to do it he says.

I read to him Leonard Andrews, he said of me this. I am a lout, I am a peasant. This is fine, it means nothing to me. My only wish is that you trust me as you've always done.

Is Leonard Andrews the name of the man saying the words he says.

No Lohan is saying the words I says.

Is Lohan a woman he says.

I don't know it doesn't say I says.

He says Leonard Andrews, I am a lout, I am a pheasant. He says Leonard Andrews, he said of me this. I am a lout, I am a pheasant. This is fine, it means nothing to me. My only wish is that you trust me as you've always done.

I started laughing I couldn't help it.

He stood up and bent over. He closed one eye and he held his buckled broken left hand under him like it was an injured deer. He says Leonard Andrews, he said of me this. I am a lout, I am a pheasant. This is fine, it means nothing to me. My only wish is that you trust me as you've always done.

Arthur started to laugh now too. Then he went serious again, he kept the red in his face, and he said the words looking over my head and his hands behind his back. He says Leonard Andrews, he said of me this. I am a lout, I am a pheasant. This is fine, it means nothing to me. My only wish is that you trust me as you've always done.

I was shaking with the laughing, the words of this thing. A feeling came on me, came up in me, light in the head and the heart with the laughing.

Leonard Andrews he says again but he couldn't say no more, he had to sit down. He was banging the table with both hands he was laughing so loud. He stood back up. Leonard Andrews he says and he went crooked, stooped down now looking terrified at the ceiling.

I says keep going and I was choking I was laughing.

Leonard Andrews I'm a lout and a pheasant says Arthur I wouldn't come anywhere near me I cannot be trusted hoo hoo ha.

He shouts his eyes closed Leonard Andrews, he said of me this. I am a lout, I am a pheasant. This is fine, it means nothing to me. My only wish is that you trust me as you've always done.

The two of us were crying, we had to sit still for three minutes get a hold of ourself, we said nothing, we had to let the laughing pass. We sat there until we were dry and we could laugh no more. And then we were quiet and I heard chairs moving on the floor, I could hear coughing.

Okay I says, I had to get my breath quick. I says okay now Arthur let's settle.

He took his tea cup in his hand and he lifted it over his head. Leonard Andrews he says looking at it.

I says Arthur serious we'll get kicked out you don't whisht.

He coughed and he said nothing then he lowered into his seat.

Ah yes he says. Yes he says. He finished his food.

I didn't go with him to meet Judith, I let him go on his own. I left the university, I went up Grafton Street and past the Tommy Hilfiger shop I went in those weeks before. I went in Saint Stephen's Green Park and I couldn't sit on the ground or the benches because they were wet. I sat by the fountain in the breeze. I heard a strange noise beside me and I seen a group of childer with a bottle of washing liquid making suds in the water. The fella dressed like a guard came walking over and I got up.

I went walking in the paths through the park. The park was quiet, this was a time people were working in offices. The park was dark too, it was the way the trees and leaves came over the paths. The breeze took the water off the leaves. People were disappearing around corners behind bushes their shoulders tense from the water dripping down their back. I had a suspicious feeling because I thought I heard someone running in a bush beside me. I heard a thing move and it was not a bird, it was too big. I got angry at myself. I was after drifting through these paths up the far end of the park now and there could have been someone in the bush looking at me and following me. Next I heard a squeaking noise behind me. I did not think anything about it then I seen what it was. It was coming off a pram with huge rusted wheels and a black skin stretched over the top of it. It was an old pram, I seen my mother's grandmother had one before. The pram passed me and went ahead of me. I could not see a baby in the pram. There was a mirror clipped to the side of it. The person pushing the pram was dressed in a dark blue skirt down to their ankles. They had a hood pulled over their head. This person was not a woman, I was sure of it, they had no arse. I started to slow in my walk. I seen the same in the person pushing the pram, they slowed too. I stopped and I seen the person stop. I thought I seen them reach in the pram. They were twenty thirty yard ahead of me. I looked about and seen no one else about, then I turned around quick and I wasn't relaxed until I seen the fountain again. When I was at the fountain I says I am an eejit, that person was a woman, why wouldn't there be a baby in that pram.

I went off back to Grafton Street and I was in the sport shop when Arthur rang.

He says where are you I been looking for you.

I says hold on I'll come down.

He was looking at a newspaper this concentrated face on him at the same table in the canteen we had our tea and burgers.

You all right he says to me.

Yes I says, I'm grand. I says did you tell her all about Leonard Andrews.

She didn't get me to say those words he says.

What words did you say I says. You can't even read.

I just made something up he says.
What she think of that I says.
He had a proud look.
I'm in the play he says.

11

My father was always a religious man and he had ideas since before I was born. They say the religious has the most childer but there was just the four in our family so it must have been the religion wasn't as big with him one point. The ideas started I don't know when. When he got married he got himself and my mother out the Cliffs and away from their people. He had his eye on a house in a corporation estate come up for sale further in nearer to Dublin where there were settled people living. These were the people he wanted his childer raised up with. And he got the house, fair play to him.

After my mother left with Beggy the ideas and the religion got stronger and the religion was the stronger of the two but the ideas were always catching up, they were never too long behind. His feelings were bad this time. It was the three of his childer went off that hit him the worst. It all happened quick. First was Margarita, married when she was seventeen one summer and gone out west. That was a hard one for him, he could not accept it. Then it was four year later that Aaron was gone, killed himself, then the next spring Beggy was off to the London Borough of Enfield with my mother. Margarita took the things she owned when she went, left the house feeling empty. Beggy took most her things too and the room she had with Margarita was like a jail cell now. Next to it the room I had with Aaron was still cluttered with the boxing prizes. It made you think it is the things people take with them makes them alive.

It was a quiet house now and I did not like that. My sisters and my mother were like the pigeons in the boxes that hadn't flexed their wings was what they were like, they made the cooing the whole time like birds. But my father was long ago spent, his head was down, his voice was down, and after my mother left another force came damping on him and you would say he was gentle. Soon it was he could talk only in a whisper but a whisper is wrong. It was louder than a whisper but lower than a voice. The voice he spoke to me with was the same voice he spoke to God with. When he spoke to me or to somebody else he saw God looking at him. It was with an eye that way. See me and sorry Lord he thought. Look at me a sinner but a tryer. His whole life my father lived like people were looking at him. He was a serious man, he was a tense man.

It got worse. His mornings and evenings were filled with prayers. I heard him first thing like the Muslims. He said his words before eating, he blessed himself a hundred times before bed. He went in and in himself, and in the television room on the back of the chair he put a picture of the dying Jesus he could not read the words of that said The Spear of Destiny. He went to mass every day but he did not go to the church that was a two minute drive, he got in his car across to the place said the mass in the Latin language of the Romans.

I said it to him how could he know what was said and he said it did not matter what was said it was living with the language of the Lord that was important.

There were the meetings after the mass anyhows would bring him up on what was said. He got in with a man the name of Mister FX who told him everything was needed to know. He got friendly with Mister FX not long before my mother left. He said to my mother Mister FX was the closest to God of any person he knew. He said to my mother a lot of nonsense. My father's religion got to my mother the same as it got to me. I am not saying my mother was not religious but she never seen the like of it the way my father went. I say thank you mother because she left me with him to see it only get worse.

After my mother left Mister FX started coming to the house. I did not like the man. The description of him is he had the wiry white and sandy hair, he wore a jacket made the sawing noise when he moved, he brought with him red biscuits and wine and he smelt of the wood in churches. In his pockets was damp paper with pictures came off on your fingers. He was a dentist but he had teeth that did not look natural. I did not trust him. He told my father they would go to Lourdes to cure my father's psoriasis of the skin. Until the time came for them to go my father was to suck holy sweet stones. Then one week Mister FX made up in his mind Lourdes was wrong, that the water the sweet stones was made of was wrong, and that a place in Turkey was the new place. I am saying this like I was out to help and protect my father but I was not. I was not out to hurt him neither but.

My father was in the control of Mister FX, I seen it. Mister FX went with him to the bishop of Dublin's house to get communicated from the church of Rome, they handed in a sheet of paper. The church my father joined that Mister FX was in was a new church would look after him, they did not need the church of Rome. There were certain things about this new church. The wine was a big part of it along with the Latin. They had the Latin bible. The bible used by the church of Rome was bad, was the same one was written by the king of England in sixteen hundred year ago. They believed the moving statues was a sign should have been seen by all Christians. Padre Pio was the Devil's field general.

My father was messing with dangerous things. What if you want to be buried the normal way I says to him one time. The whole thing was getting mad, it was hard living with, I said it to him.

This will drive me out, it is a warning I says.

My father says a strong faith is a sign of civility.

I says it's what drove mother out.

My father says your mother could not bear civility.

I thinks my mother could not bear you turning on her.

Sometimes my father himself would find it too much. Sometimes I would wake in the dust and the prizes, I would find my father not a bit of clothes on him kissing the photographs and candlesticks in the middle the night crying. And here is some words I learnt, I would say pull yourself together I says to him.

Lucky I had a job to go to. This was my prayers, this was the thing saved me. Every morning I got in my car and I went to Tunny Way industrial estate on the edge of Dublin. It was west, going west.

I worked in a plant. It was the meat business I was in. Meat was a good word for it they said. Two fellas came from Brazil to work in the plant then they left because they were disgusted. The girl who looked after the mincing said the things in the vat you wouldn't believe. I seen it a few times and I did not see bones or hoofs but I seen brains and jelly. But it did not matter once the mincer went on, was all cut down to one. The next part of it it went to the girls looked after the Meeley Burger and Spice Burger mixes. My part of it was looking after the roller that flattened the Meeley Burger meat and bringing down the press that made the meat into Meeley Burgers. The Spice Burger meat went for another pressing and a baking, the Quality Irish Mince went to other boys and girls, but the Meeley Burger was the job I done. Any shop I was in I would look for the Meeley Burger when I was getting milk and I says that was made by me.

We had a girl in the plant she was touched. She wanted to get on the bus in her whites she liked the look of them so much. Her name was Happy. It was not, it is a joke, her name was Celestina, Happy was the name one of the boys called her because he said she should have been called that. The girl called Lorna used bring her computer in the plant. It was a lap top computer. She said she stole the internet because the building next door had the internet and she could take it in through the wall. She said to me to put my head down in between the signal. I would not.

Mylo Meeley was the name of the man owned the plant. Some day he said he was going to go big, he was going to make the meat for the new religions in Ireland, the Muslims was one. Mylo Meeley looked after me, he gave me the job, he got me the money. One time he said to me to come up to the office and he had a box of dough nuts. Some other plant in the industrial estate was making the dough nuts and he got them off them. Choose your weapon he says to me. I took a chocolate one and he took a coffee one. I did not know about saying something to him because his wife said to me before to watch out that he didn't be eating sugar and cakes because he had the diabetes, she gave out black. But he was a fierce man for things that were sweet and he was a fierce man for the messing. He wore a hat indoors and he wore the wellingtons. He put his feet on the table. He says see those. He called himself a country person. He said he knew what that meant to me. I did not say anything and country person did not mean anything to me.

One summer day Mylo said to me that my father and myself were to come to his house for dinner. Mylo had a way of saying things made you feel guilty if you did not do things in the right way. I told my father and he says let's go. I says to my father are you sure you want to go. My father says why not as if it was natural. It was not natural but my father tried to act natural about it because he wanted it to be natural.

Two days before the dinner Mylo waved down from his window to come up to his office. He said to me to say to my father what he wanted to eat for the dinner. I rang my father and my father says beef and potatoes.

We went to Mylo's house and the dinner was cooked when we got in the door. When we went in the room for the dinner it was dark. Mylo had a projector machine up and he showed us pictures of buildings had been knocked down. He said his father had collected these photographs because he was in a group called the Dangerous Buildings Committee. He did not touch his food, only the potatoes. My father and me watched him, we didn't go near our food neither. Then Mylo's wife put her hand on my father's arm and says your food will go cold. My father and me and Mylo's wife ate our food in the dark and Mylo spent an hour sliding photographs in his projector machine.

After the dinner my father says to Mylo what work are you in though he knew what work Mylo was in because I was in the same work.

The meat business says Mylo.

I sold vegetables and made fountains before my psoriasis of the skin got bad says my father.

Mylo did not say anything about it, just moved to the door with us. When we were at the door the door bell rang and in came a black fat girl. Mylo said to her to take off her shoes. My father and me looked down at our shoes, we were shamed because we never took off our shoes. The black fat girl says I have lost my contact lenses. Mylo says one of them is stuck to your cheek and he moved his hand on her face. The black fat girl went up the stair and Mylo said she was their Spanish student.

She's come to Ireland to learn English and perhaps a bit our culture says Mylo.

Funny because a week later my father came out the house and he found two Spanish students hiding behind our wall. They were lying down flat on the weeds on broken glass and they were girls.

My father says what are you doing.

The two of them turned over and they were crying.

My father says stand up and he wiped their tears off their face. He says are you okay.

They said they been chased and hit by boys in the street.

I was standing beside my father and there was something not right with the Spanish students. The eyes were wide in them and one of them only had one shoe.

My father says where do you live and the place they said was a good way out. My father took them in the car back to the place they came.

The week after that my father did something I thought he was crazy. I seen him changing around Margarita and Beggy's room, I seen Margarita's bed stripped.

I went in I says to him what are you doing. I seen there was a picture of the Blessed Mother on the wall.

He says I been talking to FX and he's helped me out.

I says what has he done.

My father says FX says I am a good man and I'll make a good host.

I did not know what my father was saying. I thought a minute he was talking about the holy bread.

He says there's a girl coming from Spain in three days.

II

1

This woman was in a dream. I seen her in blue and green. The blue was the water, the green was the weed around. She came to me with the light behind her. She came to me when I was drowning. I could not see her face because of the light. I was not lifted up to the air. Maybe I am drowned then. There was no ending to this, she was in a dream as I says. I woke up and I forgot about it. Then she came again.

I got that from a book. I did not read the book, I looked at the front of it. The book was The Water Babies. I read other books. It was Judith said I should read the books. She said the reading I had was the power. Put it to use were the words. She helped me this way and now I would see and hear certain things. I would see people talking and there was always the one person holding the rest. Television programmes were stories. There was a way of knowing, the sound of them. I remembered my mother's words, the words that went up, that stopped. I remembered my father's words, the words he said to my mother. He said he knew when she was telling stories.

He knew through the walls, her words that went up, that stopped. If I listened to the people sitting out or watched television programmes I did not have to listen to the words to know. Just by the sound of them I knew.

The gift was the word. The gift, not the power. I knew this in my head. The first months in Dublin I had not stories, only words and fears came in my head. I came up the end of the summer, went through Christmas, through to the spring, all this time on my own. It was a time to think but there was no room to think. Who were these people in my head. Who were these people in my blood. Why would there be some of them that would want to spill it. It was a simple question.

I could feel the blood in me changing them early months in Dublin. Some of them that were out to get me their blood was boiling, my blood was changing. The juju man in the rooms below was screaming maybe I would scream too. Go away and be gone, let's be rid of you.

But still some people would show, some I didn't know or remember. They say it is an emptiness is the feeling, the loneliness. That was what it felt this feeling. Room to fill up with other things, ghosts and I don't know. Thoughts passed down. The beady pocket under the apron. Wisdom and ways. The quickest way to kill rabbits, a foal born on Whit Monday, bread for a poultice. Be gone be gone I would say. Sharpened sticks, titles. Let me alone I am only wanting no harm to no one. What about that fella Mac went in a hurry. Why he leave his things behind in my room, why he in such a rush to go. Maybe he was found out. He done something bad up the north of Ireland and them up there are a bad lot they will piss in your wounds take off your knees cut words in your head.

Relax yourself I would say. It is a good room for hiding. It is that indeed and there is a hiding coming to you.

Relax I would say. There are too many witnesses about. There are forty in this house, four hundred on the street, a million in the city of Dublin it was said.

I could not relax. I did not want to be hiding. I was restless them first months. I was in my room, I was hiding, but I could not settle. I could not settle in this hard city, black city, streaked with the white of the shit of the pigeons, where the roofs were rusted and spiked, where the statues with their mouth was worn. I could not talk to, I could not meet, I did not know how, I could not get at, I could not get at the people down below. I could not get at the words.

Six seven month in Dublin I heard in my room a boom and I seen through the window the sky was burning up with fire works. I says that is it. I says I don't care if the Gillaroos are lying out in the street for me I says I will go out in the street. I could have gone on there hiding in the city of Dublin but I would not hide this night. My head will be battered or I will meet some people in Dublin I says. I got in my best clothes, my shoes. I came down the stair past the doors the paint stripped off them. There were people cooking food, it will smell my clothes I says. I came down the stone steps, I moved in the street with the fire works burning above. They were orange purple and green and the street was lit, it was eerie.

The fire works were going at the river. The people were looking one way at them, I went the other way, I could not talk to people their face looking at fire works. I knew the place to meet the people was in a pub. I walked at the river until I got to a pub with a gate made of bricks outside of it. There were other pubs on the way but there were people crowding out of them so I went in this pub.

Inside in the pub I went to the counter and I asked the man for a pint of beer was what I asked. I stood at the counter, I drank the beer and I looked around. One man in the pub was shouting louder than the rest of them. He was saying yeah and hello. When I looked I seen he was standing in the corner and he was talking in a microphone. He bent down and he picked up a guitar. He pulled at the strings of the guitar and that made a loud noise too. The guitar was hanging around his neck with a coloured belt and he was wearing a leather cowboy hat. Then the man put down the guitar and he went off down to his seat and he was laughing.

I had not drunk beer a long time because I did not feel like it all my time I was in Dublin. I liked the beer I was drinking now. It was cool and it tasted of bread. I didn't think I had a thirst on me until I was supping it. When I was finished the beer I says to the man behind the counter I'll have another one. I liked the feeling came through me when I was half the way down through the second beer. I was not drunk but I was relaxed. I says I am entitled to this. I did not say it loud, I said it in my head. I said it looking around at the people. I put my arm on the counter and I looked at them.

The man with the hat came back to the corner and picked up his guitar. He sung in the microphone. The singing was loud and I did not like it when he was starting because I prefer the quieter singing. Everyone in the pub was sitting up straight or standing looking at the man in the hat. They looked happy and some of them were singing too. They were clapping to the music. Some of them had leather coats and rain coats. A man and woman kissed and then the man put his arm around the woman and they looked toward the man in the hat. A man was tapping out the music on a table. A book on the table said Ireland. At the end of the first song that the man in the hat was singing I liked the sound of him. The noise of him did not annoy me any more.

I felt the money in my pocket I thinks I will wait now, I am not a man for the drink. I says I will stay in the pub listening to the singing because I am enjoying it. I rested on the arm of a stool and I moved my head about with the sound of the music. I tapped my foot on the floor. Some of the other people were doing the same but most them were gone back talking among themself. Then the man in the hat sang a song was very popular with the people. He had his head back rolling one side to the other and he was singing with a smile.

He sings how much do I get if we say that we'll split.

Divil a bit, divil a bit, divil a bit the people in the pub sings back at him.

He sings how much is it now is written on the chit.

Divil a bit, divil a bit, divil a bit they says.

At the end of the song the people in the pub cheered the man, made a great noise. Thank you thank you the man says. He put the guitar back in the box and he left the corner to sit down at his table and have his beer.

I says to myself isn't this better than sitting in your room another night. Isn't it better than being afeard. The music was stopped but the music was still in my head and my head moved with it. I says to myself here I am look at me. I am out in the city of Dublin I am drunk. I says any the Gillaroos could come for me, I am anyone's. I thought about this but it did not bother me. My face was burning because I was smiling. The worry was in my head but a joyful feeling too. I thinks they could get me now and I would not feel the thump of a bullet because I am drunk. I would be happy dying here I says. They would think great things about me these people in the pub. The man who got killed in this pub they would say about me.

It was getting lively now in this pub. I seen I was looking this one fella dead in the eye. I did not mean to be. He lowered his head and looked in my eye like a burglar looking in through a window. He had his arm around a short old woman with glasses. He walked over toward me and he dragged the old woman with him. The old woman was laughing.

The fella says this guy will tell you.

I didn't say nothing but I was relaxed.

The fella says I've been trying to explain to my friend Kathy from America that Buttermilk are legends. Divil a bit, divil a bit, divil a bit he says, he was shouting it. He says to me tell Kathy now. Divil A Bit by Buttermilk was the fucking soundtrack to when we were young isn't that right. Every day it was on the radio. Twenty times a day he says.

The fella said this and now I heard American voices all around me. I leaned back on the counter on my elbows, I seen half them were Americans in the pub. I looked at the fella again, he was an eejit. He was annoying the Americans. Some of the Americans seen me, I nodded at them. Come here to me I thinks looking at them. Come close and let me tell you. They would think great things about me. I bought one more drink I says that is it, no more, ah yes.

Outside on the street through the gate made of bricks the people came up by the river from the fire works. There were people dressed in flags and girls with springs on their head. There were people had flags painted on their face. Some of the Americans were standing at the gate of bricks talking to themself. I nodded at them again. They looked at me then they went back to talking to themself. I moved on. I did not go walking at the river, I went up the hill behind the pub. It was dark for a mile, I got lost. I went under the church where there were more people at a pub. There was a fella leaning out a window of the pub waving and there were people shouting up at him saying he was the pope. I seen they were all dressed the same, they were dressed like clowns. Some words that was said to me when I was younger was if you are in Dublin and you are drunk don't tap into people who are drunk because they will beat you and some of them have knives. I remembered these words and I stepped around the people on the street. I came in a street where there were people gathered at a wall. They were looking at a man taking a sup from a hole in the wall, it was a font. I stayed in the group of people to see what the man was doing. He turned around to the group. He had a black mask on his face with a long nose, he was wearing dark green clothes. His mouth was hanging and water was dripping from his mouth. He said a poem about the city of Dublin's water supply and the rivers underneath and the wells above.

The group of people moved on and the man in the black mask walked in front. We walked to the back of the building with the font. We went in a dark lane and down another lane with high walls and deep steps. The man in the black mask was stooped and he was holding up his long green cloak to stop himself tripping. In the middle of the lane he turned around all a sudden. Hisshh he says. The group got a fright. He said another poem. Hish agga gog agga goggin a doo doo he says or words like that. These were old words but I cannot remember them. I was drunk as I says. I was depressed now too. He led the group on again then he walked slower than the group. He let the people pass him then he walked beside me. He lifted the mask off his face and the marks of it were pressed in his skin. His hair was plastered to his head with sweat, he was breathing heavy and he says to me you will have to pay the full amount if you want to stay with this tour. I says you are all right. I walked slower than the man and I let him get up with the group and I seen them go around the corner the other end of the lane.

The next day I came to the centre. I do not know if it was the next day. It was the same time of the year. I was depressed all this time. I am saying it was the next day. Things were set out that I came to the centre after I did not have a story to tell the Americans and it was a time I was thinking of my own people. It was early in the year all this time, it was the six seven month after I came to Dublin. It was spring is all I'm saying. The ground was wet, the air was wet, but the sun was shining and the wet was steaming. A man said the summer would be bad because the weather was good early in the year. I walked in the streets and I didn't know where I was going. I was low, it was bad times. I slipped on the slime on the kerb and I says break my skull. I was thinking to the boys in the road beat me up. Kill me I says. I don't know who I was saying it to. I was going I didn't know where, on my feet, in my head. I went through the lanes, around the square, hearing the childer screek like wild things. I went down a street past the guard station. I came back up another street. I came to the centre.

The centre looked like a church. I was not looking for a church. I think I seen a sign said something else. It said that word. The word that says it is for my people. I went around the building. It didn't look like a place you could go in, I didn't see windows. The walls were grey heavy stone and they were dirty. I went in the door but I didn't go far. A lady says can I help. I didn't say anything to her, I just read the words behind the glass. Notices was the word above. This was where I seen the note from Judith. Judith Neill said the name at the end. I am interested in hearing your stories. I am interested in hearing your stories was written in a pen. Please contact me it said. I looked at it for two minutes. My eyes went crossed and what I seen was my own face looking back in the glass. Can I help the lady says behind me. I seen my face and I seen the person I was is what I thought. I thought like this. I was a well. I thought of stories as the water. If she wants water from the well water will fill in the well. That is what I thought.

Two days after the centre I was sitting in Judith's room in the library.

Well she says to me, her hands on her knees.

This was a new place. Giant curved watery glass. A house full of stories she said to me. It was a place to make sense of the world she said. It was a place to bring sense. I would be helping her out. She said she was glad I had come. You would think it was written.

Six month on again I was back in the same room. I did not think I would be back. I was sitting in Judith's room again because of Arthur. I knew Judith would have problems with Arthur because he was not literate and he could not read the words of the play. But she thought he was good, she thought he was right. She said he was raw was the word, that the way he was saying the words made her think of the play The Cherry Orchard different. She had in fact changed her mind about what play she wanted to do now because of him. She said she was going to do another play with Arthur called Barry Lyndon. She said too she thought Arthur had a lot of stories in him. In Judith's room I thought of the well again.

I says Arthur is a well. I says there is stories in him he doesn't even know he has inside of him. He is filling up I says.

Judith sat back from her desk. She crossed her legs and smiled. She says I want to invite you and your uncle to something.

It was her Whitebrassgate theatre group she said.

She says the theatre group is only part of what we do. She says every Sunday evening I have a meeting of people in my home. Just friends of mine, like minded people. We talk about plays but we also talk about what's happening in the world. We read poetry too. I suppose you could say we tell stories. I was thinking it would be great if you and your uncle

Arthur could come along to one of our gatherings she says. Maybe next Sunday perhaps.

I says to her we will go.

Really she says.

We will go no problem, no problem at all I says.

It was a peace and calm I was feeling in that room that library. I cannot describe it. I felt that lightness again in the head and the heart. It was wet out and I was warm looking out the window. Judith was telling me I would have to read the words of the play to Arthur and I says that is no problem, no problem, because he has a great memory for words as well as stories.

I went finding him after and he was in Saint Stephen's Green Park. His arse was wet on a bench. I says you will get a cold and he says I will not. In my head I says he is worried that Judith does not want him for her plays and he does not care if he is dead of a cold now. That was his face, it was dead gone beyond, it was he did not care. You are ready for the worst I says to him and I was laughing.

I was laughing that evening, it was the mood I was in, and he was not.

I says you not excited about doing plays again.

He says I am but he did not look it.

I says let's see this new play she wants you in and he gave it to me. It said on the front of it Barry Lyndon adapted by Judith Neill from the novel by William Makepeace Thackeray. I says what part are you in this.

He says a fella called Redmond.

I looked for some of the words said by Redmond. I read it loud I says that's all the money my mother had in the world.

Mightn't I be allowed to keep it. I'm just one step ahead of the law myself. I killed an English officer in a duel and I'm on my way to Dublin until things cool down.

I laughed I says sure it's not me that's meant to be Redmond.

He was awful moody, I seen it, he would not talk.

I says what's wrong with you.

There's nothing wrong he says.

This is harder work for you than you thought I says. You will have to be learning all these words I says.

And I am cold he says.

He asked me about the day and I said it to him about the meeting in Judith's house on the Sunday. I said it to him we were meeting people and being shown the ways now like we said we wanted. I said it to him about American visitors gathered outside the library. I knew by the voices of them I says to him. They were in yellow waterproof sheets and they were brightening the rain was the way.

We slept sound that night.

I says it to him last thing we will read through the script of the play and we will have it good and you will remember the words.

I lay on my bed Arthur snoring there in the camp bed, this was the way it was now weeks him being there. This time I did not think of it when will you go. I was not depressed these days, I was not down or afeard. I thought of how it came about Arthur being in my room in the city of Dublin. This Redmond came to Dublin after he killed an English officer in a duel until things cooled down and I was in Dublin until things cooled down and Arthur was in my room until things cooled down. I was not worried now the troubles might have been caused. In my head these were old troubles. They had a sweep to them, they were moved along. All them Gillaroos might have been standing sticks burning slash hooks dripping over the side of the world and I did not care what I done to them and what they said would be done to me. They were stories, they were part of stories. They were people with hanging mouths and crooked stovepipe hats put in my way. I looked at the light on the ceiling looking down on us. It moved across, left over to right, the same as reading. When it was gone there was a weaker green light left shaking, moving like water. There is a thing called fate, I said it loud. Arthur was sound asleep he did not say anything.

I thought of it like this. It was fate put Arthur in this room with me. It was fate brought me to the centre, it was fate made me see the notice about the theatre group. It was fate made it. It was written on my hand, it was written on Arthur's hand. It was fate made stories of the things in the world.

I dreamed of the lady in blue and in green again. I did not know if it was Judith or the Blessed Mother or my own mother or the girl from Spain or no one in the dream. That is the thing about dreams. They are not stories and you cannot stop them.

2

Mister FX came to the house with the Spanish girl. The Spanish girl's name was Conchita. She had red hair, yellow skin and black eyes and she was wearing a Mickey Mouse jumper. She smelt of parma water was what she said. Mister FX had his hand on her shoulder. He says this is the girl that's going to be staying with you for the rest of the summer. My father put out his hand. He says how are you girl.

Mister FX said Conchita was up since the early hours. She had to get two planes to get to Ireland. He says Mister Sonaghan and Anthony here will look after you now. He looked in Conchita's face. He says Mister Sonaghan and Anthony will look after you now okay.

Conchita says I understand.

Mister FX says to me and my father you'll have to take it slowly with her. He says to Conchita this is a good house Conchita. It's a house of God and Anthony is a good reader he says.

Me and my father brought Conchita to Margarita and Beggy's room. I lifted Conchita's case on to Beggy's bed. My father patted Margarita's bed. It was a high and soft bed. He says this is the bed you'll be sleeping in Conchita. Conchita opened her case. She took out a cross and put it on the pillow of Margarita's bed. My father says wait a minute and he went out the room. Conchita looked at me. She smiled at me. Her mouth was bursting with teeth. She says what is your name aaaa.

Anthony I says to her.

I pointed at her. Conchita I says.

She went to her case again and took something else out. It was a picture of a man with no hair and black glasses. The picture was Pope David of the Catholic Church of Utrera. She put it at the window. My father came in with a hammer and a nail and he hung the cross on the wall beside the picture of the Blessed Mother that he put there three days before.

Mister FX had said to my father that Conchita would need a big Irish dinner her first evening. My father got potatoes and carrots and a lump of ham and boiled them. When Conchita came down for dinner she was wearing a black skirt and a black jumper. She had black tights on her legs. She had a bottle of wine in a paper bag. We sat at the table and my father said his prayer in Latin. When he was finished he says to Conchita do you say that prayer at home in Spain.

She says yes.

Then she says I don't understand Latin. She took the bottle of wine out the paper bag. This is from my parents for you she says.

My father got three cups and put them on the table. He poured wine for myself and himself. Do you drink wine he says to Conchita.

Yes says Conchita.

Your father would allow that he says.

In Spain we drink wine from when we are small she says.

When we were eating the food Conchita said she didn't like ham, she liked fish. She came from a part of Spain there was a lot of fish. It was on the sea. She said that when she was leaving her house in the early hours that morning her father had to stop his car at the train tracks to let the train pass that was bringing the fish to the middle of Spain.

My father said to Conchita he wasn't expecting her to have red hair. I thought a Spanish girl would have black hair he says.

Conchita said the part of Spain she was from was like Ireland the people said. It was green like Ireland because it rained and the people played the pipes. It wasn't many had red hair though she said. She stuck out with her red hair. From when she was small people called her the word that was the Spanish word for red.

But it's a red you wouldn't be used to seeing my father says. He was right, her hair was a dark red, dark for dark skin.

Conchita told us she had one brother and three sisters. She was the second youngest. The sister younger than her was at home. One of her other sisters was studying in Utrera. The brother was learning to be a priest in another part of Spain and the family would not speak to him. The other sister went to Mexico and the family would not speak to her neither.

I expected her to ask about Aaron and Margarita and Beggy but she did not say anything about this. After she said about her brother and sisters I seen my father was waiting too. There was water shining at the bottom of his eyes but it did not mean he was crying, it meant he was quiet and he was waiting. At the end of the dinner when Conchita had not said anything about my brother and sisters I says to myself Mister FX has told her about my brother and sisters and my mother too. I seen my father knew as well that Mister FX had told Conchita. We were relaxed.

In the morning Mister FX called at our door. He waited in the kitchen until Conchita got into her clothes for school. I did not like being around Mister FX but I was having my breakfast and I would not move. He went to the freezer and opened it, he looked in it.

He says how often do you clean out your freezer.

I says I don't know.

He came back to the table he says Anthony I want to show you something special.

He had with him a case. He clicked open the case and took out a hard leather box. The leather box was dirty and battered. He says wait until you see this.

He pulled the lid off the top of the leather box slow, his hand was shaking. There was toilet paper in the box and he lifted up the toilet paper. Then he lifted with the tips of his fingers something out the box and put it next me on the table. It was like a shell or a bit of a broken plate, a thick curved flake, grey but nearly yellow.

I says what's this.

That is a relic of Blessed Eoin O'Duffy says Mister FX.

Part of his body I says.

He says yes it is from the top of his head. I am in the process of petitioning for the upgrading of Blessed Eoin O'Duffy to sainthood status with our pontiff David. It was Blessed Eoin O'Duffy who cured your father of depression.

I says I don't want that near me I'm having me breakfast.

He says it is very special.

I says get it away from me I'll be sick.

Okay okay says Mister FX and he raising his eyebrows and his head shaking with the nerves in it, and he put the bone back in the box.

I could not eat the rest of my breakfast, I made a great show of tipping it in the bin.

Okay all right no need no need says Mister FX.

My father came in then he says everything all right. Then Conchita came in, she had on the black jumper she was wearing the night before and black trousers and make up. The three of us looked at her, she was beautiful.

My father wanted the four of us to go in his car. He said he would leave Conchita and Mister FX at the bus stop and leave me to work.

I says to my father I'm going in me own car.

We went out and my father and Mister FX and Conchita stood around my father's car. My father says come on. I laughed loud. Conchita was looking at me and she was touching the handle of the back door of my father's car. I says again to my father I am driving me own way to work.

Will you do one thing for me Anthony my father says. Will you come here look at something for me before we go.

He got in the car the driver side and he opened the door the passenger side he says to me get in. I got in and my father looked around see that Mister FX and Conchita weren't looking. They weren't looking, they were talking to each other. My father turned back around, I expected him to say something.

I says what.

He says just, and he lifted his hand.

I says what that mean.

He says don't Anthony.

I says I'm not doing nothing.

He says help me here.

It's help me now I says.

I respect you Anthony he says.

Don't make me laugh I says you don't respect me.

He says do you respect me.

What's this sort of question I says.

A shadow came in the car and we seen Mister FX looking in the window at us. My father nodded at him then Mister FX went back to talking to Conchita.

Right, that it, can I go I says to my father.

My father was pushing his finger in the radio where the music cassettes went. He says there's a music cassette in here help me get it out.

I says what music cassette.

He says I don't know it's been in the radio since I got the car.

I says I don't have time for this I have to get to work, then I hit the button beside the hole and a music cassette came in the hole but it would not come out of it. I says have you got something to stick in the hole.

My father says put your finger in.

I says me finger won't go in have you got a pencil.

He says I don't have a pencil.

I says the radio is broken I don't have the time, and I got out the car and got in my own and I drove to work.

In work a lot of the time Mylo Meeley would say to me how is your father and when he said it this time I told him we had a Spanish girl in the house like the one he had. Mylo could not believe it, he said it to me where did we get her.

I says through a fella we know.

Mylo was very interested in Conchita and he asked questions about her. He said to me was she in Ireland to learn English.

Yes we are going to teach her English I says. I said to him Mister FX had told us to take it slow with her.

What part of Spain is she from says Mylo.

I says near the sea. I said to him what she said about the fish on the train. I said to him all about how the part of Spain Conchita was from was like Ireland.

She told you all this says Mylo.

Yes I says.

She knows more English than she let on to your father's friend says Mylo.

I told the girl called Lorna in work about Conchita and she says what does she look like. I says to her she has red hair and yellow skin and black eyes.

Lorna says she sounds gorgeous and it sounds like you like her.

I says quick at Lorna she's only a young one, she's at school.

She might still be old enough for you says Lorna.

I went in the toilet and I wanted to box Lorna, that is the way I am. But I will say it again, I thought Conchita was a good looking girl, it was true.

There were certain things with Conchita at the start though had my father afeard, had both of us afeard. After that dinner that first night we thought she would be loud and my father was not a talker and neither am I. But the rest of the evenings that first week she stayed in her room and then my father was disappointed, he was worried. He went to her door he says are you all right there Conchita. One evening we were eating the dinner by ourself and my father was wondering about her, went upstair he says to her again are you all right in that room. Conchita said she been lying there reading the new catechism but then later she said it that all the girls in Spain had televisions in their room.

Later my father and me were watching the television. My father was sitting in his favourite seat, a seat that was up against the set, and I was seated on the couch to the side against the wall. He turned to me. He was twisted in his chair and he looked at me.

He says Anthony that girl comes from a foreign country. We must show her the ways to do things in this country he says.

Again I laughed loud at him I don't know why. I didn't say nothing but I thinks turn back and look at the television and think better about what you want to be saying.

Another day I came home from work I seen Conchita sitting on her own at the kitchen table. She had her hands together like she was praying. She had the look on her face that was serene, it was a look of patience. She says hello Anthony your father has gone to get me something.

My father came in he had two books in his hand, his work books he called them, he had them for when he sold the vegetables. He put them flat on the table and he opened them.

This is how I ran my business in the old days he says to Conchita.

Down one length on every page of his work books my father had different things written meaning different vegetables, an x for cabbages, a circle for potatoes, a v for radishes,

I could not remember all of them. Down the length beside the vegetables he had numbers, the only things he could read was numbers. Some of the vegetables had numbers over them.

Sometimes my customers would pay on credit and this is the sign for credit he says to Conchita, and he pointed to a v that was long on one side. He says and different customers is different numbers of dots see here he says. Jim Fulton is four dots, Missus Jeane Quinn is nine dots, Matt Hanlon is four dots with a circle around them, Eblana guesthouse is two dots he says.

Why do you use the dots says Conchita.

It is the way with business says my father.

When did you sell vegetables says Conchita.

It is something I done says my father.

I says to Conchita he started before I was born and we lived in a place called the Cliffs. The soil there was good for growing vegetables. And our people in the houses built glass houses and people used come from miles about to stand on the top of the cliff and look at the glass houses wasn't that it father.

My father was red in the face, he says it was my work Conchita, every man has a job, that is how things is in Ireland.

Conchita went to her bed and I heard noise coming from behind the door. I says to my father what is that noise. He said it was a television. My father had got another line put in that morning in Margarita and Beggy's room for Conchita. He'd skipped mass for the first time a long time waiting for the man to come put in the line. It was not good skipping mass but it was something couldn't be got around he said.

He says here help me with this now. He opened a press and he took out a music cassette. The music cassette was a mess, the tape inside of it was spilt out.

Can you fix this he says.

I says what is that.

He says that's the music cassette was stuck in the car that time.

I says what would you want with that.

He says I want to fix it.

I says give it here. I took a pencil and I put the pencil in the teeth in the music cassette and I turned the pencil around. The tape went back in the music cassette.

My father put the music cassette in the radio in the kitchen.

I says you don't listen to music.

He pressed the button on the radio and the radio played a terrible broken noise, we had to turn it off, it was a symbol.

3

On the Sunday myself and Arthur got the bus out to the part of Dublin Judith was living. It was over the river and over the canal. We got the directions. The houses out that way were a dark red and a light brown, some of them were orange. Judith's house was a height of three floors, had a deep roof. The door was covered in a sheet of stripes. The sheet was to guard the paint of the door.

Judith opened the door with a glass of wine in her hand. She had her hair tied up in a ball with two long needles cut crossway through it.

She says welcome fellows, welcome welcome. She says I am sorry about my pampas grass it's so over grown.

Me and Arthur seen where she was pointing was a tall clump of yellow plants with feathers on the top.

Arthur says there are a lot of bushes and trees in the area maam.

Judith says yes. On a damp summer's evening it's magnificent. After the sun's come out you just breathe Arthur see, and your lungs fill up like this.

In the hall in the house she had more plants, tall green plants growing up out their pot nearly touching the ceiling. There was a tall green plant on the landing too. On the wall going up the stair were pictures of Chinese women whose clothes were gold and face was paint.

She brought us down steps and in a room. The room went the length of the house from front to back. It was a big room but it was dark. She would not put on lamps because it was still the day. She went out the room to get us wine. Arthur walked around in the room. Judith came back and stood in the door, a smile on her face.

Arthur was looking in a glass case. Inside it were ornaments.

White Chinese porcelain says Judith. She went over to him. She says it's all from the same part of China indeed it's all from the same kilns including this figure of Mao which is centuries newer than the oldest piece in here. Roy is the person to ask about all this. He'll be here later he's very interested in oriental art.

I says to Judith Arthur was interested in the antiques himself. He used sell them.

Arthur would not look at Judith. He stared in the case, his hands in his pockets, a hump in his back.

Were you in the antiques trade Arthur says Judith.

No says Arthur.

I says don't be telling lies.

Arthur says I sold a bit of shit.

I says to Judith he sold antiques in all around France and England and Germany.

I picked up oul shit and sold it the next oul place says Arthur.

He walked about the room again, he touched a gramophone record player. He says I seen these before.

Judith says that was my father's. I still have some of his records though they're very scratched.

Arthur touched a piano, he says I seen one like this before too.

Another heirloom she says.

Belonging to your father he says.

Yes she says. She sat down at the piano and put her wine on the piano. She leaned her arm on it.

Arthur says is that him. He was pointing to a picture on the wall of a man in a green suit. The man was leaning back in a chair. It was like he was falling asleep in the chair, he was not bothered. He had brown hair but he looked old. His face was very pink and it was rough.

No that's not him says Judith laughing. We call him Mister Toad she says.

Do you have a husband says Arthur.

No says Judith.

Is there anything else in the house was your father's says Arthur.

Quite a bit of it she says. The house itself was his. It's changed in some ways and in other ways not at all. This long room you're sitting in used to be two rooms, a drawing room and a dining room, before I knocked down the wall between them. My father late in his life got rid of a lot of the house's contents or at least shoved them up to the attic before I brought them down again. Other things I managed to retrieve one way or another.

Arthur says was your father a rich man.

Judith says yes if you counted all that he owned but most of his life he did struggle. She says he was a very interesting man, he was born in eighteen ninety six.

She said to us the story of her father. She said it as the people in her group started to come to the house. She didn't want to bore them she said but she said the story anyways. The people that came were Professor Michael Gregory, this man Roy, a German woman name of Izzy, a lesbian woman name of Pam, an angry man who wrote plays name of Stephen, two women who painted paintings name of Sheila and Melody, a poet name of Nuala and a man who practised dancing, married in May he said, name of Don.

The story of Judith's father was he was called Gordon Neill. He lived in Judith's house nearly the whole of his life. His mother was an invalid since Gordon was born. She had two more boys sitting up in her basket wheel chair but after that she could not have any more childer. When Gordon was sixteen his mother died. She died in her basket wheel chair that was turned over on a stone floor. It happened in the house and one of Gordon's brothers said years after that Gordon and Gordon's father killed the mother but the brother did not mind it because the mother was very sick. When Gordon was eighteen the first war started. The young men on the road left their homes with cakes made by their mammies and walked down the road and turned off to fight in the war. In their gardens they shook the puppet called punch at their mammies and laughed at their mammies and there were flags in the trees. They were saying don't worry mammies we will be home for Christmas and we are fighting for Ireland. Gordon's father was seeing all this through his window, he says to Gordon come and look at this. Gordon's father says if this war is still going on in two year you will be the same age as these young men and you will be wanting to go to fight as well. And in another two year and another two year your brothers will be going to fight he says. I do not want you going to fight in this war you will be killed he says. Gordon says to his father do not worry yourself father I won't be going to the war. He says nobody has to fight in this war if they do not want it. These fellas on the road think it is the thing to be doing, they are mad he says. I am not mad he says. These fellas are not thinking for themself, I am thinking for my self. I am thinking of the terrible thing has been done to our country and I am staying here he says. The father was happy Gordon was saying this, he knew he would not go to fight. The next few year the war was going on and hundreds of people were dying. All this time Gordon was going to the university and half the people in the university were going to fight in the war and half of them were saying it was madness.

They talked about it in rooms. On Saturdays and Sundays and other nights Gordon brought his friends from the university to his house. Gordon and his friends told poems and talked about what was happening in the world. They wrote their own poems as well. They wrote about boats' masts, fairies and Ireland. Sometimes they brought in women to the house. They got the women from hospitals and schools and they had sex with the women. Gordon's father did not like this but he put up with it because it meant Gordon was not fighting in the war. When the war was over Gordon finished in the university. The year after this the fight for Ireland started. Gordon and two of his friends said they would fight for Ireland in Paris. They went to Paris but they did not have a good time. They said they were ignored. They went to Italy and they were three year in Italy. When Gordon came back to Ireland Ireland was its own country, it was not ruled by England.

The evening in Judith's house we were drunk. The wine went to our head. Arthur and me sat back from the group of them, we sat by the fire place. I seen the man in the picture's green suit was moving when I looked at him, that was the effect of the wine. The chat went on the whole night.

Professor Michael said he drove his car in a street in a town and the town ended but the street went on and there were new shops for a half a mile on the street. He said all the shops were empty, there was no one in them, no one selling things and no one buying things. At the end of the shops was a shopping centre with a roof of glass.

Stephen said the shopping centre would be a good place to set off a bomb. No one would be killed but it would say something about the shops better than all the shops being taken over by the bank. He said the shops would be so badly built that the roof of glass would fall in and the shops would fall in as well.

Pam said you could not know if all the shops were empty and people might be killed.

Professor Michael says not this again we're going we're going, and he shook his head and he leaned over laughing and the rest of the group were laughing too but not Stephen who had white hair cut close on his head and his head was going pink under his hair.

Judith says shall I go down to the cellar and she went and came back with two bottles.

Nuala said if everybody in Ireland when they were dead gave their money and their house for tax to Ireland and every child in Ireland had to work hard to get money and get jobs would it make Ireland a place that was fair.

Professor Michael said there would be nothing different if this was done because the poor childer would not want to get educated anyhows.

Stephen said it was not true to be saying the poor childer did not want to get educated.

Pam said the poor childer would want to get educated if they knew it was a fair fight to get the top jobs.

Nuala said if the childer of the rich and the childer of the poor were starting from the same in life it would be a fair fight and the poor would change their mind about the education.

Stephen got more angry says you're making grave assumptions Michael. He says Nuala it's also not true to say that one hundred per cent inheritance tax would turn the heads of the working classes that's a patronising position to take Nuala Nuala listen to me he says that's a gross generalisation that's an assumption Nuala that the working classes of this country are not interested as it is in bettering themselves through learning and that it would take some major upheaval to turn them on to the idea, you simply don't have any understanding of working class communities how many working class people do you know Nuala very few is the answer and how can you therefore make your argument which is based on the assumption that the working classes have a dim view of education.

Stephen Stephen come on now says Nuala listen to me I'm taking the working classes' side, you're not listening to me.

Stephen was standing up from his seat.

Judith says I have to say Stephen I'm liking your bomb in the shopping centre idea.

Sheila said she didn't want to be stepping into this even though it was healthy but she said that she wondered that if everybody in Ireland that died had to give their money and their house away in tax for Ireland would it have made any of the people in the room be different.

Melody says knowing that taking a career path would involve an even bloodier dog fight than has to be fought already would be enough to send me careering in the other direction thank you.

Izzy says yes a meritocratic society would be a rampantly capitalist one because the only idea that meritocracy promotes is that there's a pie to be eaten.

Stephen was still standing he says listen to you. Guff guff all of it he says. And you're saying the working classes are dogs he says to Melody.

Melody said she did not say that.

Stephen says you're saying a level playing field would generate a dog fight. And who would be the dogs.

Everybody in the group hit their knee and was laughing and says Stephen.

Stephen says I tell you dogs was what the pigs in Kevin Street called my folks just because they thought they could just because my folks were market traders.

Stephen Stephen they says.

Stephen says Melody or was it Sheila you think art is going to solve the problems of this country. Art and art alone. I'm sick of this twinkly twinkly bull shit you think we can bring about change by throwing a bit of paint on canvas that won't even be seen or writing a few lines on a page that won't be read well I tell you I'm writing my thoughts I'm turning them into art all right but I'm out on the streets I'm pressing my words into people's hands I'm bringing my theatre to the people I'm in people's faces I'm on the television.

Judith said what does it be saying about Ireland when the people of Ireland congratulate and love two blond singing canary boy twins that England is laughing at and voted out of their country.

Don said what is worse the books about real criminals or the books about criminals that was made up in someone's head.

Roy said if any of them watched a film about a boy and a girl and the girl likes the boy but the boy doesn't like the girl and the boy works in the television business he said all of them would be skipping home happy.

4

Conchita would come in the house from the school she would say to my father how are you Mister Sonaghan how was your day. And even if my father done nothing in the day he would tell her what he done. If he been meeting with Mister FX he would say I been meeting with Mister FX, if he been thinking he would say I been thinking of Julian's revelations of divine love or I been thinking of the Holy Ghost telling Blessed Angela that God loved her more than any other person in the valley.

For two weeks in the middle the summer it rained heavy non stop and no one could leave their house. The gutters were choking Conchita said. One of the days we watched a foreign man. We had not seen him before. He had moved into the house behind our house. The rain stopped an hour and he came out his house and that was the first we seen him. He went on his kitchen roof with a satellite and he was bolting it to the wall. The rain came heavier than before and he put a bag on his head. When we went looking next there were ambulance men on the roof. They took him away and we heard the man got electrocuted and it burnt through his nerves. He would not be the same man again. It upset my father and Conchita awful, it upset me. My father and

Conchita prayed a whole evening for the man. Conchita said she would not ask for a satellite for her television.

One of the Saturdays my father says Conchita says she wants to go into Dublin on the bus Anthony will you go with her.

I says to myself she goes in Dublin every morning of the week but I did not say anything to my father because I wanted to go in Dublin with Conchita.

On the bus Conchita sat at the window, I sat in beside her. Nearly the whole way she looked out the window. Her eyes were squinting. She said the cloud was lifted she said the sun was out. In her part of Spain she said it was rain and sun the whole time and two rainbows. Two boys were spilling marbles and old washers down the floor of the bus. I was stopping the marbles and washers with my foot. I says yes to Conchita the whole way, I was not listening. The boys were looking over the seat, one had a small white face and was smiling the other was looking straight in my eye and bending down with the marbles and washers. I says sometimes you cannot be sure about certain boys this is why I don't get the bus. Conchita was looking at the window she was frightened of the boys. When we were coming into Dublin Conchita turned to me she said her father was an angry man. She said her father found her with a book about what happens in people's thoughts and head. She said to me she knew from this book if a man pissed in a bottle what that meant and if a child held a dog by the chin what that meant. She said it was something that was interesting but her father did not like it. She made the move in the air with her hand the way her father hit her and she said pp pp pp with her mouth.

Conchita said she wanted to go to Grafton Street. I did not know the streets this time, I did not go in Dublin much, but I made it like I knew the streets. My father did not know the streets neither but he wanted Conchita to think he knew them, he wanted her to think I knew the streets. He says to me before we left the house do you know where to be going, do you know which streets. I looked at Conchita in the street now, I wanted to be doing right, I respected my father. I says to Conchita Grafton Street is this way but she knew the way.

When we got to the end of the street we were walking in Conchita says to me does your father hit you. I didn't know what to say, I was embarrassed. I says no, it was the truth, but I didn't say if he hit me I would hit him back.

She said that was another thing she learnt off that book, that the religious people liked hitting people including themself.

In Grafton Street Conchita said she wanted to go in a shop sold clothes. She found the shop, it was a huge shop silver inside with loud music coming out of it. I said to Conchita I would not go in then I went in and came out again, I didn't like the men's clothes and I didn't like the music. Conchita was in the shop twenty minutes then she came out she said she didn't like the girls' clothes neither.

We went across to McDonald's, we sat down in a corner with Cokes and a quarter pound and a chicken burger and chips. Conchita said a strange thing, she says a true test of how much you love someone is if you imagine strangling them to death.

A thing I seen in Conchita was every word she said she said it quick but in her head the words were slowed down. I seen her mouth saying the words. Her mouth moved around the words before she said them and after she said them. When she was concentrating her eyes were closed over and the eyes jittered under the skin.

She says if you see in their eyes as they look at you for one last time a look of being confused and suddenly sadness and if what you feel then outside your imagination is sadness and you want to go to that person you imagined murdering and hold them and they do not know where this feeling in you of wanting to hold them close to you came from but they are happy it is happening and the sense of this comes to you and you want to hold them tighter and with more love then that means you truly love them.

She opened her eyes she says do you think I am strange.

I thought sometimes she was strange but I says I don't think you're strange but I says you are thinking a lot about killing and fighting.

She says I'm very normal.

I says you're good at speaking.

You mean English she says.

Yes I says.

She says I will tell you a secret.

I waited for her to tell me the secret but she would not tell me the secret.

When she was finished her chicken burger and chips she went up again and got a banana in a cake. She ate into the cake then she lowered her head forward and her eyes opened up.

I says are you all right there.

She says uunh and she looked at me. She says this is the same taste in my mouth when I think about Catherine Labouré.

I knew who Catherine Labouré was I seen pictures of her dead body, she made the Miraculous Medals. I thought it was strange to be saying and then Conchita put her hand on the top of my arm and pinched it. I did not mind it but I did not know what to be saying.

Conchita put down the cake and went up and got a coffee. She drank the coffee and put her tongue outside her head for to suck air in her mouth. When she was finished drinking her coffee she took her phone from her bag and she looked at it.

She says Anthony I am meeting my friends from the school now. My friend has sent me a message to say she is in the city centre.

I says do the other girls in the school show the boys in their house to one another or are they shamed of them.

Conchita says I would not say that but these are my friends and I said I would meet them on my own I am so sorry.

She put her hand on my arm again but she did not pinch it this time.

You're welcome I says.

Do you say you're welcome when someone says they are sorry she says.

You do I says.

Oh that is a beautiful thing to say she says.

We went different ways outside McDonald's. We said to ourself we would meet back in the house because Conchita was not sure what time herself and her friend would be finished meeting. I walked away out of Grafton Street, I did not like the noise. I went down at the river where men sold their badges and sold poems. I looked up the river with the sun in my eyes. There was a smell of earth in the air and there was a seal in the river. Past the chimneys and the smoke was the Phoenix Park, some way in that direction. It was a way I could have walked but I didn't know about it then. I could have lied down in the trees with a girl, I would not have cared if it was wet, I like that smell. I am thinking of girls the whole time, there are many girls I would go with, I am thinking of Conchita too. I would like to be doing things, hold their face, it is stupid, but I would not go after young girls the same as Arthur went after young girls.

Some time I should have said something to Conchita. I should have said that my father was only in serious in the religion in the last two three year. I seen it is a religion of violence, I seen it is a religion of pain and tears, and many take their violence from the violence done to Christ and do not feel shamed of the religion if that is what you are, but the violence my father learnt he learnt it from others and that was why he hit my mother. But I would not have said the thing about my mother. And I would not have said about where he learnt the things he left behind. I would have said my father is a man of ideas, and there is some that fill up with water and there is some that are buckets that draw up the water but my father wants to be the weight that goes below to what has settled, and in this way I grew up, and this is where I grew up, and everyone comes from somewhere.

5

Madame Neill's salons they were called. We learnt the name off Pam the lesbian woman. We came up to her at the back of Judith's house. She was smoking and she looked at us suspicious. She had small ears and the lamp above her head lit the hairs on her face. Her trousers were tight around her legs and she struggled getting her box of cigarettes out the pocket. She says to us a smoke anyone.

Arthur says yes missus if you don't mind it.

She did not say much. Arthur and me got the fit of giggles, we tried to stop ourself. She blew the smoke out her mouth thin and flat, she looked at us. She says what do you think of Madame Neill's salons. She said it in a certain way.

Arthur says they're good and I says they're good.

Good she says nodding.

Then she says well don't worry about anything and she threw her cigarette on the damp grass and turned into the house.

We found it hard keeping up with the things were said in Judith's house. Everyone talked the same time, people were shouting, the wine given out made us drunk. Angry Stephen would stand up and people would say sit down.

Stephen waved his arms he would say no one can really say he says.

He says the church owed people more than just.

He says in my day are dangerous words.

He says the arrogance.

He says the government the people the ways the reasons.

Sit down Stephen sit down says Professor Michael and Izzy and Melody and Don.

Will we go Arthur would say to me in a low voice.

I tried reading the play Barry Lyndon with Arthur. I sat down with it in the room in the house I would say some words to him. It made him restless. We didn't get far most the nights because he would end up rubbing his skull, hc would walk around the room he would flick things. I would say stop flicking things he would keep doing it.

I says what is wrong with you.

He says it makes them feel good it doesn't make me feel good.

I says well something might come of it.

One day I came out with words of my own for the play I says it's a shite play.

He says it is one word for it, we laughed.

We went on with it anyhows, but Arthur was getting more difficult, more restless. Another day he disappeared altogether and I got worried. The evening came along he still hadn't returned. It turned pitch dark still no sign of him. Ten o'clock came he turned up at the door.

I says where you been I don't like you making me feel like a worried oul one.

He says I been out looking for a job.

I says have you been drinking.

He says no I went looking for a job then I went drinking.

I says what pub were you in would have you.

He says a place full of Russians.

I says let's go there.

The place we went was a beautiful wooden place, had varnished dark wood inside of it and ship's brass windows. The thing we seen about it was three people were smoking but smoking was banned like this. Up high in a corner was a television showing music videos but the sound was turned down. Down the end of the pub an old woman with purple hair was sitting across a very small table from an old man. She had the old man grabbed by the hair of his head and she was cutting the hair out his nose and ears with a scissors. The man had his mouth open and he was saying ah. The bar man and some others were turned to them and laughing.

There were not many others in the pub and me and Arthur got two pints of cool bright beer in strange tall glasses, were big in France Arthur said, and sat ourself down near the end near the old man and woman.

I says to Arthur where did you go looking for jobs.

Different places he says. Three of them were garages.

Any others I says.

A motor cycle shop, a hardware shop, a Spar he says.

You just went turning up at doors I says.

I asked to speak to the boss man he says.

What did they say to you I says.

No jobs here and that was it he says. Two of them said I'd have to get a CV letter, I turned around and said fuck off he says.

I says why you looking for a job all a sudden.

He was about to say something then he said nothing.

Then he says I don't know.

I says and you missing the whole day and me worried again about the Gillaroos had got you. There was another one of us and one of them killed you heard of it.

He says Anthony it is time to start looking in the real world.

I says the real world.

He says yes.

I says what you talking about the real world you're in the real world.

He looked at me he says you know something.

I says what.

He says you cannot take your drink. One sup and you're gone.

I says I am not gone.

He says Anthony.

I says what.

Look he says.

Look where I says.

Look at me he says. He says I'm going to push on.

Push on I says.

Do me own thing and stop trying with all this, this wasting he says.

Go back to your old ways is what you're saying I says.

No he says. Get a job, get ready, push on, push through he says.

I says the world will push harder against you it's not worth it.

Then it's time to fight against them he says.

There's others will fight harder I says.

Don't I know he says. But I am ready for a fight he says.

I says what you mean with that.

A man with a shaved blond head and no eyebrows walked up to our table he said something we did not understand it.

I says to Arthur what you mean you're ready for the fight.

Arthur looked at the man, he says no to him shaking his head and putting his hand over his glass. The man slapped his hand on the table like he was putting down a hand of cards. He lifted his hand and he smiled at Arthur and he walked out the pub.

I says to Arthur what you mean it's time to fight.

Will you shut up he says.

We looked at the table where the man had put his hand. There was a sticker there had a picture of a fist packed tight and the veins showing and the word Ultras under it.

I said to Arthur something I hadn't said a while, I says Arthur what sort of danger are we in what is it. What you mean with the real world I says. Do you know something about the Gillaroos.

He looked at me quick, he was about to say something quick too. Then he put his beer to his mouth, blocking his mouth. I seen his face change, it loosed up. He put his drink back on the table and he moved his left hand away from my sight, on to his leg.

We heard a sound this moment so loud we got a fright, we had to duck our head. We looked over we seen a Russian man shouting in a microphone, he was testing it to see how loud it would go. The bar man beside him was pointing in the air with the television control and the television sound came on. We looked at the television over our head we seen the music videos were still playing. Next the fella with the microphone sang words in his language that were coming on the television.

We sat through one song then another fella took the microphone and started singing another song, he was brutal. The music was so loud we could not think, it was hurting our ears. Arthur made the move with his hand to go and we got up.

When we were passing the end of the bar the bar man waved us toward him. He said something but we could not hear him. He took the television control and brought the noise of the music down. The people in the pub were not happy. They shouted about it, some of them looked angry, the bar man shouted back at them. He put two glasses on the counter were like shots glasses but bigger, he poured vodka in them. He leaned close to us, we leaned into him, he says on the house. Me and Arthur looked at each other. The bar man leaned in again he says tonight is the last night here tomorrow we close and I go back to my home land.

We would not turn down an offer from a man, we would not turn down free drink is the truth. We took the drink but somebody was not happy us getting it. A man came up to the bar beside us, he was giving out to the bar man. He had blond hair long and done like a woman and little eyes close together. We knew it was us he was giving out about because he looked at us blood eyed and looked back at the bar man. He was short, only up to my shoulder, but he was built strong. His hands were waving, he was very worked up. The bar man was calm, he spoke back at him in his language.

The blond man's voice went louder, he thumped his fist on the bar he turned to us he says fuck you.

We were not expecting words like this, we stood straight we went the other side of the stools to him.

The man went at it again he pushed his chest out he beat it with his fist. He says the same he says fuck you Irish fuck. We didn't know what was going to happen and next he went at Arthur, he swung at him.

Arthur went straight back at him, he went for his throat, he pulled himself toward the man and he head butted him.

The man fell back but Arthur had a hold on him, he pulled him closer to him, he boxed the man on the side of the head. The man took Arthur by the flanks and now the two of them were locked in each other. They were turning one way then the other, the two of them red in the face, their mouth spitting and dribbling. Soon as I had a clear go at the man I had a shot, I punched him in the belly, but there was no give there, my fist hit into damp leather, the man was built like bricks.

This stage the bar man and another man with a shaved head were out on the floor and they got Arthur away and they got us all separated. These two big lads were keeping the blond hair man with his mouth bleeding coming at us again and the woman with the scissors and the rest the crowd in the bar were shouting black abuse at us.

Arthur was raring, I had my arm around his shoulders I says settle. His breathing was quick I says calm now Arthur.

He pointed to the blond hair man he says to him you got the wrong fella.

Come on Arthur let's go I says.

He touched his mouth he says to me there blood there.

No I says.

Is me throat burst open he says the fucker had his fingers in me mouth.

Your throat's not burst I says come on.

He felt his mouth the whole walk back to the house. He was distracted by it, he walked into bins. When we were seated in the room he kept saying the question what was that man's problem. He fell down on his camp bed he says that man didn't like the look or sound of us and he doesn't even speak our language. He doesn't even understand about us says Arthur.

The two of us wondered what could we do and we said to ourself what was there we could do. I said one thing we could do was that he should not abandon me now. He might have brought trouble along with him but he should stick with me now if there was trouble. We're in this now I says to him, come with me where I go, you help me I help you I says. The next Sunday we were back at Madame Neill's salons. We said we would keep going to Madame Neill's salons. Push on, push on with what we had. We would keep going and something might come of it we said.

6

Every morning every day that summer Conchita was in the house the weather was bad. When I woke up and looked out my window I seen clear sky but when I looked out the window in the kitchen the other side of the house I seen thick clouds. When I left the house to go to work I seen the line in the sky there was clear sky and thick clouds. When I got to work it rained heavy in sheets. The water jumped from the ground, it turned to white spray off car roofs. I did not know what clothes to be wearing these days. There was sun one minute heavy rain in the next minute. But it was always hot in the air so I wore my shirt, I got wet, I did not care in the end.

In work in Meeley Meats a girl found a way to the roof. This was a great discovery they said. On lunch some people in Meeley Meats used go in their cars to coffee restaurants or some people sat on a step in the side with their sandwiches on their lap and looked at the field of flat concrete and followed the yellow lines on the concrete with their eyes and played a game. After the girl found the way to the roof the people who sat on the step went to the roof. People were not allowed smoke on the roof but people went smoking on the roof anyhows and people brought their tea on the roof. People liked the roof because they said it was the beach. The surface of it was grit on a sheet nailed down. In the sun it heated up and it twinkled when you moved your head. Always in this summer there was one end of the roof in a puddle of water and it was the sea. The people in work lay down on the sheet their cheek on the grit sometimes their feet near the sea. When you stood the mountains was over the side of the roof.

One day in the summer I went on the roof with a boy name of Joe and a girl her name was Babs. These people had troubles, all people in the work had their troubles. Babs had sun glasses on her face. We did not know how a dog got on the roof. The dog was playing in the water then he ran around the back of some chimneys and structures. Joe said he was not surprised there was a dog on the roof and Babs said she thought it was normal. They said the place was a dirty place. I looked over at the chimneys but Joe said he thought the dog fell over the side of the roof because he was excited. Babs says don't say that Joe but Joe said that was what he thought and the dog did not come back around but we did not look over on the ground to see was he dead.

Joe and Babs says let's enjoy the sun while we can. They lay on the grit and put their tea on it. I did not like to lie on the grit, I liked to sit on the wall on the side of the roof. I liked to look out in the country. Sometimes I drove out that way. One time in the snow I went out beyond the motor way and I looked in the sky I seen the sky was yellow above Dublin. Many days this way the puddles were ice, it was where the wind came in. In a field were trailers. Even with no wind the trailers shook gentle side to side. They were windy wagons was what was said, it was a television programme for childer.

Joe and Babs talked and said we would be out of jobs the way things were going. I did not hear this thing before. I looked at them I says is this true. They said things were bad in Meeley Meats. The two of them did not look worried about it. Babs had her sun glasses and the two of them were laid down. They smoked cigarettes, the sun was shining on their face, there was the smell of perfume had come up.

The door in the roof opened and out walked Mylo Meeley. Joe and Babs got a fright they tried to hide their cigarettes but Mylo says it's all right it's all right. Mylo took out a cigarette himself and had sun glasses himself. He stood looking over at the mountains tapping his cigarette on his cigarette box.

Joe says Mylo there's a dog in your factory. Mylo did not say anything, he turned his head to the side for a minute then he looked back at the mountains then he walked around the roof sucking his cigarette with concentration.

I says to people in work do you think we will lose our jobs and some of them said they didn't know and some of them said yes. I did not want to be losing my job, I did not want the factory to be shutting down on Mylo because Mylo looked after me he looked after a lot of the people. I said about Mylo and a boy name of Conor looked about him and he looked at his work and he laughed. I says to the girl Lorna what he smiling about and Lorna said Conor seen something in the week before made him shocked and made him laugh. I says what he see and Lorna said Conor went in the store room and he seen Mylo with his trousers down pulling at his mickey and some girl the other side of the window. She said the girl the other side of the window was standing there because the glass that side was like a mirror and she was putting on her make up for the morning. Mylo was looking at this and the girl had her mouth open putting on her make up. Lorna made the shape with her mouth of the mouth on a girl putting on her make up. Lorna said she bet the girl stopped at the window every morning the same time going to work in the industrial estate and every morning Mylo pulled at his mickey looking at the girl.

After I heard this about Mylo I looked at him and the work different. It was getting in on me, I don't know. I went on the roof with tea or sometimes to walk and sometimes Mylo seen me going up more than I should have been going on the roof. He did not stop me, he looked away. He even went on the roof himself more and more. Sometimes it rained heavy and he still be up there when I be running in escaping out of it and he would walk around the edges and the rain coming down and the drips off his nose.

I will remember that summer, it is only not long ago. I will remember it for the work gone bad, for what happened Meeley Meats, and I will remember it for Conchita in the house. I will remember and I am remembering it now. I remember this summer for the rain and the heat, the rain pelting, coming down in strings of oil down the side of the house and the blue weak light what it was. Them blue hot rainy days stuck in of doors and the strings of rain that were white with the houses behind them. The light by the kitchen window, a weak light.

I remember Conchita sitting at the table her shoes off, her orange brown and pink and grey socks her feet under her on the chair, her eyes in the light that was weak. Her eyes were black but in the light in the window they were brown and gold and she was looking out the window in at the air and the sky. And that is the picture of it I remember, I will remember. I seen it, I am seeing it now, I will bang my head thinking.

One day I said it to Conchita because I was thinking about it, it was bothering me, I says what age are you Conchita.

She says I am eighteen.

I says quick I am twenty two. I says bluh bluh gluh gluh, I said stupid things. I did not think Conchita would say she was eighteen, I was not expecting it, I thought she was younger.

I says you are eighteen.

She said her father and mother kept her out of school when she was a young thing because they wanted to teach her about the religion but later she went in school but she was the eldest in the class, she felt left out of it she said.

I says oh. Oh oh ah is what I said.

I opened my gob I says I know lads went back in school too they went back in because they left it when they were young but they went back to do their exam.

I heard these words come out my mouth I says stupid eejit myself, I thinks she will think the things I don't want her to think if I says I knew lads left school and went back did their exam. I didn't want her knowing nothing about my people, I was shamed about it.

I said to her the truth I says I did not know these boys who left school and went back.

Conchita looked at me strange.

I says it was Aaron knew them boys, they were two friends of Aaron's.

I said Aaron, now Conchita talked about Aaron, I did not want to talk about Aaron but it was better than talking about the people I was from.

Conchita says how did Aaron die.

I says he killed himself.

Conchita says how did he kill himself.

I said it to her that he hanged himself.

Conchita did not say anything.

I says some boys wanted to get at him and it made him depressed.

Conchita did not say anything.

It went on like this. I said about Aaron. What I said was these boys heard he was good at the boxing and they put it to him on blank DVDs that they wanted to fight him. I said it to her that my father would not allow Aaron fight these boys but Aaron went on anyhows. He lost his boxing licence because of it. I said this made him depressed and my father went mad at him, made him more depressed.

It was the first time I said these words and it was good for me was the truth of it. I says to Conchita you aren't just good at the talking you're good at the listening too.

She was embarrassed, she turned her head, I looked in her ear.

I says your ear is like the inside of a shield.

She says a shield.

I says a shield.

I says your ear is like the milk the inside of a pot's been boiled to the bottom.

I says no your ear is like the light in a cup that looks like a sea gull.

I says your ear is like the inside of a shell.

She says that's what my name means it means shell.

I says shell, repeating it.

What does your name mean she says.

I don't know I says.

Then I says no, Anthony is the saint of lost things. That is what I heard I says.

She says I like this name. I like your father's name too. Aubrey is a word for red brown no she says.

It is a name has got him in trouble I says. Some people think it is too grand a name.

Which people are these she says.

People who knew him I says.

Conchita was confused but I could not say more, I was quiet.

Tell me more about Aaron she says. Who were these boys who wanted to fight him she says.

I do not want to talk about him now I says.

I think back on all of this with Conchita I think what I would say if I was talking again. I would say you are too good at listening that is the problem. I would say words to her would have nothing to do with who I am and who I came from. Normal things and I would say to her she was beautiful. It was a summer a lot was done but I could have done more and better. I am remembering it, I am shamed about the lot of it, I am shamed or maybe the word is paining me.

At the end of the summer Conchita was joking and she made a shape of a V with her hands the bottom of her stomach. She had a harsh laugh in her. She said she could never go to certain countries because her name meant also little cunt.

7

Arthur was getting down in himself. Some days I thought he was normal and then he done something I seen he was right the way down. One time we walked past the church I been told was the black church. If you hopped around it three times you would see the Devil, I said it to Arthur. Next he was off hopping up the path hysteric to himself. When he got to the end one side he stopped. He was holding his waist. I went up to him I thought he was laughing. He was not he had a stitch and I seen he was depressed.

One day I heard bangs distant in the air. The next day I heard them again. It was getting into the end of the autumn. There was drizzle and there was the feel of the dampened down fires about too. There was the smell of guns. Soon it was all you heard was bangs. We heard a loud bang when we were sitting in the room. It sounded it was in the lane near by, the echo went through us, hurt our ears. I flicked off the television then I flicked it on again. Arthur said did I get the television with the room. I says no I found it dumped on the street. We talked about the television for ten minutes, we did not talk about the bang. One morning we were walking in the street we heard a bang as loud, we moved on quick. Near the house we heard another bang distant. Arthur grabbed my hand, he hurt it from holding it so tight. He wouldn't let go. I tried to move my hand, loosen his grip on me. Then he hooked his arm around my arm. I walked on he was still holding on to me. I stopped I says to him stop being an oul woman. His face did not look right, he was not looking at anything. I says are you only seeing the Devil now. We walked on again I says to him serious Arthur you're making me afeard stop being an oul woman.

One evening I says to Arthur remember when we were standing on that bridge in the middle of Dublin those weeks ago and you were pointing down the river and you said you used come in Dublin down that way, was it something you used do a lot was it something our people did coming in Dublin or did they keep out of Dublin did they know their way in Dublin speak to me Arthur I says.

One time I was in a shop I was getting some things. I seen a newspaper, I never read the newspaper but this one I read. I seen at the front of it it said Carnage In Clongar. There was a picture of the face of my cousin Paul Gillaroo with it. He was looking grown up but he had blood down his face and he was giving angry looks in the picture. He was looking me in the eye from the picture, it was like he was looking from a DVD. I read the words under the picture it said turn to page six I read the words it said a group of savages from the Gillaroo clan descended was the word on the village of Clongar where some of the Sonaghans were living they laid siege to the village were the words it was a picture of devastation both factions went at each other armed with planks of wood, baseball bats, pieces of scaffolding, kitchen knives, crow bars, bicycle chains, hurleys, golf clubs, broken broom handles, broken patio slabs, slash hooks, meat hooks, nunchuks, samurai swords, antique Zulu spears. I looked for who was killed but it didn't say if someone was killed but a lot of the mob was badly hurt they had to get sewn up in hospital.

The boy in the shop says there's no reading the papers.

I put the newspaper down I picked up my bag and went to go out the shop. Before I got to the door I turned to the boy I says to him how far from Dublin is Clongar.

The boy didn't say nothing then he made a face like he didn't know and didn't care about it.

And fuck yourself too I says to him.

In Judith's garden was a bomb shelter we could have hidden in. When she showed us it didn't look like nothing, it was a brick building the same height as me. It was dark that end of the garden. Judith's garden was on a hill and this was the bottom of it. The only light we were getting came from the strong white lamp fixed to the back of the house. Somewhere was the noise of a river moving.

The brick building had one door and no window and the back of it went down in an angle. Judith had a key with her, she put it in the door. She says I like to keep this locked just in case, you never know who might use it as a den.

The inside of the brick building there was a nail in the wall and a torch hanging from the nail. Judith put on the torch and we walked behind her down steps. Over our head was the angle. Down in under the angle and down below the ground was a room big as Judith's kitchen.

Judith moved the torch around the room. See how big it is boys look she says.

There were shelfs on the walls and bunk beds, two of them, four beds all, was like a trailer. There was a sink and a tap.

Judith says well I guess it's what you might call these days open plan living. My father Gordon built this place as a bomb shelter in nineteen forty she says. He thought that if he needed to he could live in here with his wife at the time Ellen and my half brothers until the war blew over. He thought the Germans might bomb Dublin. He thought that if they did bomb Dublin poisonous gases would linger in the air for years after. But he was silly. Of course the Germans had no interest in bombing Dublin, Dublin was not important enough.

I did not know why we were brought to this place. I looked at the bunk beds. Judith was standing in water on the floor in her bare feet. She had nearly fallen over on her high heel shoes on the grass so she had taken them off and thrown them in the dark in the bushes.

She says guys you'll be interested to know I have great ideas for this space. I want to turn it into the stage for my summer garden theatre. It would be perfect. I want to take off the roof just lop it off like the top of a tin can. I want to cut the slope of the garden into a steeper gradient so it comes right down to the floor here. Seats will be set into the ground above. So from here to the back wall will be the stage. I will have trenches cut either side from where the actors will enter and exit and from where the scenery can be wheeled on. What do you think Arthur. Can you see yourself throwing your arms about and projecting your voice into the air above from this platform she says.

Arthur says it'd be a lot of work.

Yes I know says Judith.

You'd need to be getting the JCB to do the work he says.

Oh I know that says Judith I imagine I'll need engineers and plumbers and electricians and all sorts to help out.

Arthur says the air is damp this place there's the smell of black rot.

Yes says Judith. She lowered the beam of the torch. Let's get back into the fresh air she says.

She would not let up about her Whitebrassgate and her play Barry Lyndon. One time when the group of them in the house were after talking themself tired and looking at their bellies she said to Arthur to say a bit of the play Barry Lyndon.

Professor Michael says woah oh and everyone looking at their bellies looked up.

Judith says as you know ladies and gents Arthur here is going to play Redmond in Barry Lyndon for us and he's going to play it brilliantly. And Anthony is helping Arthur out by going over the lines for him so that he'll remember them but Arthur won't have a problem because he has a great memory.

Professor Michael says have you got a story for us Arthur.

Arthur did not say anything. I seen he looked sick because we were all after drinking very heavy drink and the man name of Don was smoking hashish.

Professor Michael says any stories at all Arthur I hear you're a great storyteller.

Professor Michael looked at Judith but Judith wasn't looking at him and she wasn't looking at no one but her face was happy. Professor Michael didn't look at no one now neither he looked shamed was in his face.

The German woman Izzy says what about some dialogue from the play perhaps the two of you could show us.

I says missus I don't know any the words I just be reading them to him.

Judith says even just do us a line Arthur, any line your favourite line. She says to the group watch it watch the shape it's all in the shape you'll see what I mean.

Arthur didn't say nothing. He had his hands on his knees, his head was low.

Ah Arthur don't let me down says Judith and the group laughing around her.

Ah leave him be if he doesn't want to do it says Pam.

You'll need to get over your shyness Arthur if you want to perform in front of others says Judith isn't that right Anthony.

All a sudden he stood up. Everyone sat back in their seat. He put out his arm and pulled back the sleeve of his shirt and turned his hand so the palm was toward the ceiling. I waited for words about Redmond or Leonard Andrew but he did not say any words about no one he made a noise like an engine a whine and he says missus missus.

Then Roy took a post card from his shirt he said was from Don after he got married. He says listen to this, Konstantinopol with a K the twentieth of May. Dead to the world. No infernal muezzin cries to wake us. The air is pregnant with the smell of rose and saffron.

Judith says in my ear why don't you guys go and make yourselves comfortable in the room upstairs I have ready for you.

Professor Michael came over the other side of me, put his hand on my shoulder. He says to Judith is the DVD player still hooked up in the room.

We went up to a room the very top of the house, under the beams, Professor Michael showed us. There was a bed made up and a couch made up as a bed. Me and Arthur sat the end of the bed and Professor Michael put a DVD in the machine. He could not get it to work, he pressed the buttons, then he got it to work. He says you'll enjoy this film both of you. Judith wouldn't be very happy about me saying this but she took her play pretty much from this film. Just watch it and you'll have no problems. The film is based on a book but I wouldn't torture you by giving you the book. He says enjoy it now and make yourselves comfortable up here. The couch is very comfortable, my son has slept on it he says.

He went out the room and down the stair and the film was playing.

We did not like the film. It was about a man, Redmond, who went to fight in the war. When he went to the war we turned the film off, it was a boring film. We stayed sitting on the bed. We listened at the noise down the stair under the floors. The group were talking again, they were talking loud. The voices came through but we could not hear the words. We sat ten minutes looking at the television that was turned off and listening to the noise down the stair.

I seen a door to another room, I went over to it. I looked at Arthur, he was not looking at me, he was not interested, he was looking at the wall. I turned the handle of the door and went in the room, it was a room had a rotted wood window the glass in it wrinkled. The room was full of green plants, their sleeping leaves were on my hand. I looked through the window I seen the lights of other houses in the dark. I came back in the bedroom I says to Arthur do you think everyone else in all the other houses is sitting in groups like Judith and her friends.

I pulled out the chair was under the table where the television was sitting, I sat in the chair.

Arthur was flat on his back on the bed, his eyes were open.

He says where will we go.

We sat on the seat and lay on the bed and listened to the voices coming through.

8

There is a very interesting story about our people. I think of this story now I think of my mother starting again with an old story of hers. That is what this story is, it is another start to another story. I think of this story I think of my father. I think of him kissing his left thumb. He is looking to the sky and now he is turning his nail and crossing his head, his lip and his heart.

I think of him standing in a field. He is stripped to the waist and the last of the challengers is lying pounded in the dirt. I see him walking away and the crowd cheering him hitting him on the back, the crowd passing money under his head and the crowd dying away around him and him walking on and looking at his thumb, his left thumb, and seeing it bitten and bleeding and dirt in the wound and him spitting it clean and licking it clean and his tongue shaking and his hand shaking and him hearing a voice, a calling, saying this is not for your people this is for me and taking off his belt and hitting a stone and hitting a stone and walking and hitting a stone and hearing no more of the fighting or the old ways I have a special path for you.

I think of the men that came to the Cliffs to take Teresa back. I see them pulling her, peeling her away from that unnatural mark. They are haring off through ploughed black muck and hanging drizzle, they are going over tar past yellow teeth and yellow lights to the mountains.

I think of Aaron the southpaw. I think of that weapon he had. Coiled to spring it was said.

I hear the words of the Gillaroo spiking the Sonaghan saying they are a people always pointed the wrong way.

And I think of Arthur and I think of his hand and I think of his scars, and I think of the time I first heard this story of our people, sitting in Judith's garden, and all a sudden I knew it all I thought, why this terrible wound was done to him, why he had this terrible fucking monkey hand, it was clear as if it was sitting in front of me.

It was a time it was quiet, there was no talking loud. There were none of the others, there was just Judith myself and Arthur. We were seated on wood chairs at a wood table under a heater. We had not taken heavy drink. It was a beautiful clear evening and the ducks were disappearing from the country over our head.

Stories of the Sonaghans came out our people's mouth and were said to Judith's father. They been through many mouths and the last mouth was Judith. We learnt Judith had a mouth on her indeed. She had caused a lot of harm to her father in his life time but she was making up for it after he was gone. She been a bad daughter she said, she would have thrown herself through glass she would have taken a sharp bit of glass she said.

Will you go on out of that talk says Arthur.

She had her troubles like the rest of us, but the trouble she was when she was a young one and she was wild was serving her to the good now she said, although it was a pity her present troubles were out of her hands to mend because she loved a married man and he would not leave his wife but that was a different story she said.

Let me get this straight she says you two are uncle and nephew through via because of whom.

But anyways she was the way she was back then she said.

She says I caused my daddy such grief when I was young but he was a fine man. I've come to realise that I am my father's daughter, we are the same person. He was pushing the boundaries and I could not appreciate it at the time. In fact he was so much more daring than me, he was a pioneer and a radical. You would have liked him fellas. He touched everyone he met, he was a great listener, he knew where the soul and salvation of this country was, that was his greatness.

He had worked like Judith in a university and many years ago he went out in the field and he spoke to the native people of this country. He set out to write down every part of our culture, he filled note books with wisdom and story and song. He thought it was important in a time when no one else did. Judith was working through the note books, copying the stories, bringing them into the store of knowledge. There were such riches it was the most enjoyable work she ever done she said.

She had the note books out from a box on the table. They were in the damp in her attic too long and they had mushrooms on them once but it was not the note books themself was important it was what was in them was important.

Where were you from originally she says.

We came out of Melvin I says.

Melvin the same as the Gillaroos Arthur says.

That's right says Judith, she says Melvin.

She been on the look out for stories about the Sonaghans and she found our name all through the note books, but we are one of the biggest names through the country and through England.

She read words in the note books, she said about wagons and tents and the Blessed Mother tinware panboxes churching and ringworm and seeing pooka in farm yards.

Do you know about these things she says.

I heard of some of them says Arthur.

She put the note books to one side and she stirred up out her seat and twisted the handle on the heater, made the flame glow bright and blue. Now she says.

Arthur says can you lower that flame.

I've only just turned it up she says.

No can you bring the pole down to a lower height so's the flame is close to us he says.

No I can't says Judith, it's at a fixed height.

No bother, no bother says Arthur.

I think of our stories now I think of an old man saying them because they are stories older than Judith and older than them books. They are stories could have been said by the man said to Judith's father the stories but they are stories could have been said by a man going back further than that. They are stories for wild bright sparking fires and dying clear low fires.

The Sonaghans were the fish were put in the lake in Melvin by God himself so it goes. He put them in one by one with his own hand. The left hand is the Devil's hand and God would not use his left hand and he put the Sonaghan fish in the lake by holding the fish tight in his right hand. When he was holding the fish in his right hand his thumb pressed in their left side and when he let them go in the lake the mark of God's thumb was burnt in the Sonaghan fish's left side as the sign they were the fish were from God. When the Sonaghans grew to people the mark of God stayed with them on their own thumb. Because the mark of the thumb of God was on the left side of the fish, when they grew to people it was on their left thumb that the Sonaghans had the mark of God. Favoured was the word, chosen was the word.

They are words would be said by the old man jumping off his seat on the ground, he has only two teeth there is smoke and buckets near him. He spits on the ground he says and we are the ones is chosen by the Lord the others is dirt. He laughs loud showing the old holes in his teeth. He says you see it today and it's the special sign of the Sonaghan so it is. Look at any of our left thumb. Take a look at me own look at it. See it now. The print on it is different to the print on all me other fingers and the other thumb see it. See it he says.

In her garden under the heater in the dark Judith says come now and look at this. She opened one of the books on the table on one of the pages. I seen the two thumb marks of a man must have been made using burnt wood. One was written left underneath it the other was written right.

See how the lines in one print are so different to the lines in the other says Judith.

The right one was loops getting smaller and smaller one inside the other, the left was different it was true.

It's an S shape do you see says Judith.

I could see it clear now it was pointed to me yes it was an S shape. I looked at my own thumbs I seen the exact same, something I never seen before. My right thumb was loops, even my fingers was loops, but my left thumb was an S. The lines of it gathered at the top and moved together in a swerve and back and back out again. I was standing under this gas heater and lamp looking at it, Sonaghan or sinner I did not know.

Judith says well Arthur let's see yours.

Arthur says I don't have it.

She remembered his hand was deformed, I'm sorry she says.

But Arthur opened his left hand anyhows. The thumb that was his toe didn't look sore no more but it looked strange still. It still did not look like the thumb of a person it looked like the thumb of a monkey, looked like a toe what it looked.

I seen Judith was embarrassed was the look, she was shamed.

Arthur says see maam not every one of us gets it.

9

There were men in the work one of the days they wanted to talk to us all. They were in clothes made from toilet paper, was tissue was said. I says to someone what is it about they said the men said we were to work normal they would be around to every one of us and talk to us one after the other.

I was working normal, I was at the press. Later in the morning one of the men came to me he says how are you. He says can we have a minute with you sir.

I seen they were taking people in a room, he took me in the room too. The blind in the room was shut and the light was on. The man says take a seat.

The man did not say anything to me he says only can you stretch out your hands good man.

He said to me to hold my hands up and open and flat. He looked at the tops of the fingers he says can I see the other side, he looked at the other side too.

Good he says.

There was a black box in the room it had a gap in the side of it, the man said to me to put my hands in the gap. He turned off the light in the room then I seen my hands in the gap in the box were lit up in a blue colour. I got a strange feeling looking at my hands. The man pulled in in the seat beside me he looked in at my hands too. They did not feel like my own hands, I was floating around them.

The next bit of it the man turned the light in the room back on. He says keep your hands in the machine for a moment. He says now take your hands out of the machine and try not to touch anything as you do so. Keep them hovering in the air like a magician or like this like a dove good man he says.

The man went to the box he took up the paper at the bottom of the gap my hands were in. He crushed the paper and threw it in the bin. He took off the gloves he was wearing he put them in the bin too. He put on new gloves. He pulled more paper from a pipe he put a sheet of this paper on a table.

He says float your hands above the paper and try not to touch it if you can.

My arms were sore and my hands went down.

He says try not to touch the paper if you can.

The man opened a box. He had glass and wool in it. He took a stick from a glass, he rubbed the stick over the palms of my hands and up my fingers and thumbs. He touched the stick off a bit of cloth twenty times.

He says I'm sorry about this, he took a needle from the box as well.

I says I don't want you sticking needles in me.

He says I won't be sticking any needle in you. He says I'm just going to give your nails a quick clean it won't take long.

He went under my nails with the needle, I did not like it one bit.

When all of it was finished the man said to me to wash my hands well and he showed a way to wash my hands.

I says I know how to wash me hands I don't need to be told it.

He says you must take time to wash your hands and you must wash every part of your hands.

I asked them on the floor when the men were gone who else got their hands looked at the same as me. There were eight of them on the floor all of them had their hands in the box but it was only me got their nails cleaned out got told the way to wash their hands. I could not work for the rest of the day my hands were shaking I was angry.

I went up to Mylo was how angry I was. The thing I seen about his office was how clean it was, I never seen this before. There were things gone from it, things put away, the walls smelt of fruit.

Mylo was angry too he says I know I know.

He said to me to take the rest of the day off work I was disgusted I was with the men, treating me like this.

It was the Thursday of that week I came to the factory and there didn't look like nothing wrong outside of the place and then I seen things were wrong inside of it. In two seconds I seen things were not normal, nobody was working, you would have thought there was something going to happen. People been saying things were bad a long time but it didn't stop them doing their work, now all things were stopped, something was wrong.

I says to the girl Lorna what's wrong.

Lorna says it's not good I says what is it she says we'll hear soon enough.

I seen my press it was turned off, I seen all the machines on the floor they were turned off.

We were waiting on the floor we looked up at Mylo's office. We were looking for a change in the light, something moving. A fella came on the floor he said he looked in the store room and other rooms he couldn't find Mylo nowhere. He said he would go up to Mylo's office he says this is not on. He went up the steps and in Mylo's office then he came out.

No one there he says.

We were stood about, there were doors into machines and we wondered did we have to start turning off lights. Somebody says take what you can, charge your phones, but nobody moved, nobody took anything was said serious, even jokes were said.

Then Mylo came in the main door his coat still on him. He was sweating but he was smiling, his brown hair was blown.

He says sorry.

We waited for him to say something but he was breathing heavy. We waited for him to breathe normal and steady then we seen the smile go from his face. We lowered our face to look in his eyes, he would not look in our eyes. The group of them went toward him, I stood where I was. They put their arms around him, he fell into them beside him, in their arms he went, they caught him. He floated, he was loose, they walked with him to the other side of the floor. I seen him he was crying he says I have let you all down. They put him on a seat they says Mylo things will be okay. Someone fed him a bar and put their hand under his chin to catch the crumbs then someone took him to a pub.

We sat about outside saying I don't know about it. We were all out of a job and people were shocked. Where would we go they were saying. Someone said we would all get jobs again, we said where. He says I'll get all of you jobs. Someone else said what about Celestina who was touched. The boy who brought Celestina to work and home every day brought her home he said he would talk to her mammy. Someone other says I'm going to the pub with Mylo, that is the right idea. Everyone said goodbye to everyone else, people were squeezing the others' shoulders, but nobody moved, they all stayed and talked, nobody could believe it what just happened.

I could not stand about hearing this the whole day, I got in my car. I didn't like it my job was gone but I would get another one I'd get it on my own. I came out the industrial estate I says there are some of them will not get jobs again, there are some are handicapped. I came up the fly road I went in the sheets of water. It did not feel natural to be going home to the house this time, I said I would drive. I came on to the motor way my tyres were purring. I didn't like music but I put on the radio I heard men and women talking, they were talking about animals having sex. Mylo was going to get it from his missus now I says. Deserved it he did, it was funny but it wasn't funny. He was cheating on her or if he wasn't cheating on her he was thinking about cheating on her with the one in the window. He should have been thinking about his business I says. Too much going on for these people isn't no one like me going to help themself clinging to these people isn't that right I says I will go until I hit the buffers all of them, all them country people on the roads.

10

Conchita wanted to go in Dublin I wanted to go in Dublin with her. I says to her this time I will drive the both of us in Dublin, I will find a place to park the car. She said she did not want to go in the car she wanted to go on the bus. I said I would go on the bus. I went out the house with her, I said to her I would go in the shops with her. I looked at her I says we will go in the shops what shops will we go in but she said she did not care about the shops, the shops in Dublin were not like the shops in Spain. At the bus stop she says bye. I says we only just got to the bus stop why you saying to me bye.

She says I'm going to meet my friend from school.

I says I'll go with you.

Conchita says no.

The bus came and she got on it, she had a card she put in the machine. She rushed on the bus she didn't look behind her, she shot up the stair of the bus. People were getting off the bus, a slow old one and an old man. I went in around them, I went in at the machine. When I was in the bus I felt in my pockets I didn't have the coins. I says to the bus man I have a friend up the stair I'll get the coins off her give me a minute.

The bus man had sun glasses on him he says you fucking will not.

I says to the bus man don't you use language with me.

He says get off the bus now or I'll ring the guards.

I went to try get the coins anyhows I thinks to hell with him. The bus man turned off the engine and came out his seat.

He says get off the bus now.

A man in the bus says to me get off the bus and the other people on the bus were giving out, another man says don't be holding us up you.

I walked back up the bus toward the door and the bus man went back in his seat behind the glass. When I went past him I thumped the glass my fist, I was annoyed with him. I got off the bus, he shouted at me. I went to shout at him, he closed the door on me. It hissed, I says don't hiss that thing at me.

When Conchita came home from Dublin it was late in the evening. I says to her did you meet your friend in Dublin she says yes.

She says was there trouble on the bus.

I says what.

She says the bus driver said on his microphone that he was sorry about the trouble.

I says what trouble he say.

She says he said a man jumped on the bus and he made people afraid.

I says what else he say.

Conchita says he didn't say more.

I says what else he say, Conchita says he didn't say anything more, I did not believe her.

Conchita stayed after school some of the days to be with her friend. I said it to my father about it, my father did not say anything about it.

I says to him she's staying after school with this friend, she's coming back to the house late it's not good, my father said nothing, he made a noise.

Conchita met her friend the Saturdays too and one of the Sundays. I says to her when I meet your friend Conchita.

She says she smiling at me she says I don't know.

I says I don't mind to be talking Spanish I'll learn the Spanish I'll talk to your friends. I says to Conchita is your friend from Spain.

She says no my friend's from Ireland.

I been thinking about the trouble on the bus I says to Conchita did you say to your friend about me on the bus.

She looked confused, I didn't know if she was putting it on. She says no I didn't say anything about you on the bus.

I says to her don't say nothing to your friend about me on the bus.

In the evening Conchita went in at the television where my father was, she says Mister Sonaghan I'm going into Dublin to meet a friend for a few hours. She said nothing to me and she left the house. It wasn't until one o'clock in the morning she was back in the house, I was lying in bed listening, I was brewing.

The next morning we had a row I says to her why you been keeping your friend away from me she says you wouldn't be interested in my friend.

I says your friend isn't interested in me.

Conchita says what do you mean don't be stupid you don't even know my friend.

I says your friend thinks she knows it all about me and don't be telling lies you told your friend about me hitting the bus. I says your friend is the same as the bus man she thinks I'm the scum on the earth so she does and she been telling you lies about me and that's the reason you been keeping your friend away from me and me father you're shamed of us so you are.

Conchita says I don't understand I says fuck yourself I says.

After Conchita came back from school she says I'm sorry Anthony. She says are you sorry.

I says I haven't got nothing to be sorry about.

She says well I am sorry. I would like you to meet my friend she says.

I says you sorry you bring your friend to the house to meet me.

Conchita says okay I will.

I says I want to meet your friend I want to talk to your friend.

She says I will bring my friend to the house.

On a Monday so I was at home, nothing to do, I been driving all day. I was not expecting Conchita to bring her friend with her to the house this night but this night was the night she did it. My father was away for the evening this night, he was away meeting with Mister FX and their group doing charity was their thing on this night. Conchita knew this, she knew this for a while Monday evenings, and this why she brought her friend with her to the house on this night. She could get away with it she knew and it was something she wanted to be getting away with because her friend was not a girl, it was a boy.

Conchita says Anthony this is my friend Fintan, he teaches me English in the school.

This fella was standing there in my television room. I was shocked and I did not like it, I was expecting a girl. I looked at Conchita she was smiling up at this fella. I did not get up from my seat. I looked at him once and quick then I looked back at the television.

He went to sit in my father's seat and Conchita sat on the couch. He'd had drink and so had Conchita, the minute they sat down I could smell it off them. I thought what kind of a fella is this fella. I looked at him the side of my eye, I seen the way his knees were high and pointing in the air he was a tall fella.

He says anything good on.

I says there's nothing on.

What are you watching says the fella.

I did not say anything because he could see what I was watching, I was watching the inside of the stars' houses.

He says hey and I looked over at him. He was leaning over at me. He had his hand out he wanted me to shake it. I will shake someone's hand if they put it out I shook his hand.

Anthony right he says.

I looked at Conchita she was watching the stars' houses on the television. I says to him yes Anthony.

We looked at the programme, after two minutes he says are you really watching this mate.

I did not say anything to him he says there's something better on the other station.

I says to him nothing then I says it's a funny name all the same Fintan.

Fintan I seen had the hair and beard like Francis of Assisi and a sick look like Francis of Assisi, thought himself looked very smart but he was not a religious man, and Conchita was not a religious girl.

Conchita says Anthony you still have beer in the fridge don't you.

I says we do.

Conchita got up, the fella followed her, they didn't ask me could they have the beer. They came back in the room with the beer, they sat on the couch. The fella says cool house I like it, I like the statue in the kitchen.

When they were settled we watched more of the programme then I pressed the button on the control to turn off the television.

I says I been thinking about what you were saying and it's true I'm not watching this programme it is shite what it is.

The fella was confused and I knew he would be confused.

I says we don't watch television in this house.

Okay says the fella.

We sat in the quiet I let it one minute.

Now I says what we do in this house is we tell stories.

The fella says cool, okay, he laughed about it, he was drunk.

I looked at Conchita I says isn't that it Conchita.

She did not know what I was saying, I says I will tell you a story because that is the thing in this house, it is a house of storytelling.

I turned in my seat I says I'll tell both of you a story now it is about a farmer his wife and a gentleman came by on the road.

Get off my land says the fella.

I says do not be interrupting me you mustn't interrupt when I'm telling a story it is important.

Sorry he says. He says go ahead, then he opened his mouth he burped.

And do not be fucking burping at me neither I says to him.

Conchita says Anthony this is not normal for you and she was right about it I was angry, I was angry she was taking advantage my father not being in the house bringing a boy in the house.

She says to her boy friend Fintan I'll show you something, and they both went out the room.

I did not like it one bit them moving about my house without me saying but I stopped myself jumping up after them because it was getting if I pressed on him too much it would come to blows, I knew it, I let them out the room.

Then I heard the back door open. I knew they were standing outside and the fella was smoking a cigarette. Then they came back in the house but they did not come back in the television room, they went up the stair.

I got out my seat I went out the room, I went up the stair I stood outside Margarita and Beggy's room. I did not hear

Conchita and the fella there, I stood outside the toilet I heard them there. I heard noises, kissing. I heard joking and whispering. I thought I would get sick on the floor, I didn't know what to be doing. I put my hand on the wall, I looked at the door of the toilet. I could not stand there long the things in my head, I went back down to the room I pressed my head in my hand.

After ten minutes I heard the two of them come down the stair laughing saying sh. The fella did not delay in the house, it sounded he was swept out the house because Conchita knew what they done was disgusting but they were laughing as they said goodbye one another all the same.

I says to myself Conchita do not come in the television room and she did not, she went straight back up the stair to wash herself and go to bed.

In the morning I got up early, I went to the kitchen got my breakfast. Conchita came in the kitchen, she had the look on her face was bold almost fierce like she would not be saying nothing about anything. I thought this was a face she was putting on, it was an effort.

When she turned to leave and go to school I says to her there's a word for you.

She did not ask me the word or answer me back, she moved to the front door.

I moved behind her to the front door I says behind her I will not say the word, this is a house that fears God.

My father was away at mass for the morning. When he came back I was waiting for him. After mass he would have tea and bread and I waited for him to be sitting down and having his tea and bread.

I says to him something funny happened last night when you were out doing the charity.

He says oh.

I says Conchita didn't come back until late and it wasn't until you were out doing the charity she came and listen to this are you listening.

Go on he says.

She came back with a fella with her I says.

Oh he says.

Do you hear me I says.

I do he says.

They were up there in the toilet and they weren't wiping their arse I says.

My father didn't say nothing, he folded up his bread looked more serious in the eyes but he didn't say nothing.

Are you listening to what I'm saying to you I says.

Anthony stop shouting he says.

You and your stupid ways and look what you've brought in the house I says. You are slipping man is what you're doing. This is not your ways. See what happens when you try to be like the fucking buffers on the road. You bring a buffer in and they rule you I says.

My father says don't you be using them rude words like buffers.

Buffers is what they are and buffers is what you're not I says.

My father went to get up and go in the garden.

I says go on fuck off buffer.

My father says Anthony serious don't.

I says I'm going out in me car.

My father says go on fuck off.

I says how am I going to stick it now in the house with you around no self respect I says.

Get another job my father says.

I says I will not get another job hear me. Hear me I says shouting at him and he gone in the garden. I opened the top window I says shouting louder no pride and self respect.

I sat at the table boiling, cooling. I closed my eyes, a pain in my head, I had a thought that was strange. It was I was at the bottom that dried lake in Melvin and I knew it what side I was with. I breathed, filling.

I went back to the window, I had a feel of something. I seen the garden, the walls that my father painted white because the grey bricks made us all depressed, the broken plates nailed to the bricks. I seen the fountains he made and the pillars he made himself of concrete. Some of these pillars were on the tops of the walls. Down the bottom these walls and pillars and plates was my father in amongst it, kicking the grass that was now tall. I seen a look on him I hadn't seen a long time, a change coming on him, coming on quick. It was like all that was damping down on him was lifted. His head was lit and twitching, he was blowing mucus. He was shifting one foot this way and back, one foot that way and back.

I went out the kitchen nice and slow, I locked the door.

I heard the back door banging and my father coming pounding and skittering on the floor. The kitchen door took a thump and moved.

Aaaah he says, it was not words.

Go on animal you fuck, get it out of you I says.

Aaaah he says, and the door started to split.

What you going to do I says. You going to nearly kill me like you nearly killed me mother I says.

Aaaah he says, aaaah, aaaah, and I left him, I left him there to burn out.

I went out driving. I went aimless about, I was not thinking. I was running low on diesel I says if I run out of diesel I will siphon it. I wondered what I would do I wondered would I stick things out would I sell cigarettes, but I did not wonder too long. I had my mind made up what I'd do from now and there was no wondering about it.

By late in the evening I had a bag packed up. I didn't have much in it I didn't have much anyhows and a lot of it I didn't want anyhows. I hadn't seen Conchita since she came back from school, soon as she came in the door she went up the stair. Not long Conchita would be gone from the house, I think she had a week left in it but I would not be waiting to see her go but I wanted to see her one last time. When I was ready I went in to her, I did not knock, I opened the door.

She was on her bed watching the television but when she seen me come in she took one look she sat up stiff.

I sat the end of the bed I says how are you girl.

She did not say anything.

I says I want to say something to you and I want you to listen to me careful.

She says okay.

I says relax there now and listen to me.

She would not relax she looked afeard of me but there wasn't no need to be afeard. I would not hit her but I seen the bone under her skin behind her ear I could have grabbed and torn the hair floating there and held her and spat the words in her ear but I did not.

I says I am going to be leaving this house for good in the morning first thing. I need to be writing something for me father for him to know about it, I need to leave it down somewhere like on the kitchen table. But there isn't no point in me writing these things for him I says because he can't read, that is the way with a lot of our people do you understand me. I says so I am going to tell you now the exact words I want you to say to him so listen very careful what I am going to say. Are you listening I says.

Yes says Conchita.

I says you say to me father for me that I am gone out of here and this life you understand me.

What do you mean says Conchita.

I says tell me father I am gone to meet me people. Tell him the Gillaroos, say the Gillaroos, that is their name, I am gone to join them because they are me people. Tell him they are living their life the real way and I am gone to the town called Rath. You understand all this I says to Conchita.

She says no.

Rath Rath the Gillaroos remember it child I says. Tell him I am gone to live the life that is true.

11

We were in Judith's kitchen. We stood beside one another, our back to the sink. I was very warm, I was hot. I was holding a glass of cold water and the glass was misting above the line of the water, I was looking at it. The door of the kitchen opened and Stephen came in. His head was red, his head was always red under his short white hair, red as the scarf he had on him. He been shouting all night but now he did not look angry. He looked like he was gathering himself, winding down. He had his hands in his pockets. The ends of the scarf went the length of his arms and in behind his hands. I seen over him in the hall that Judith was standing by the front door with his coat. His lips were tight and he was looking at us. He stopped in front of us and he was going to say something then he didn't. He looked down at the floor, he took his hand out his pocket and he shook my hand, he shook Arthur's hand, he says I'll see you lads. Then he left the kitchen and he left the house. Later we heard myself and Arthur were the only people in the house Stephen said goodbye to. We heard he said he would not be coming back to Judith's house and salons again, he really done it this time they said.

The next day was the last day me and Arthur were in Judith's house too but I did not know it then. I did not know a lot of things about it at the time, that I would see a lot of things that day I would not put out of my mind. We stayed in the house in the top room again and all I knew in the morning was I wanted to get up and get out that house quick with Arthur.

I woke at ten and I shook him awake I says let's be going.

We snuck down the stair then Arthur says I need to be getting some tea for the road me mouth is dry.

I says if we have tea we'll be here all day just take a sup from the tap.

Arthur says I want me tea.

I says you'll wake them.

Arthur says what about it, we'll have our tea say goodbye and go.

All right so I says.

We were seated in the kitchen having our tea then Arthur says did you hear a noise last night, screaming.

I thought about it, I remembered I did hear screaming in the night, it woke me then I went back asleep. The screaming came from Judith's room where she was sleeping with her boy friend Professor Michael.

Arthur says maybe the two of them are going through troubles.

I says that was some troubles.

A few minutes later they came in the kitchen and Professor Michael looked shook. He walked tense like his body was tight. Judith had her arm about his back. She helped him in a seat at the table. She sat beside him, wiped the side of his mouth with a cloth. She looked at us and gave a dart of a smile at us.

She says well drama boys.

Arthur looked at Professor Michael he says are you all right sir would you like a cup of tea.

No wuh says Professor Michael and he lifting his hand at us and speaking through a down turned mouth.

He won't be eating or drinking anything right now says Judith. He just needs to sit up for a while.

I says sleep is the only thing for it that's the only cure for me.

Judith says oh no it's not what you think. Michael has had this problem for a long time and it's not brought on by alcohol.

Arthur says is it fits he gets.

Judith did not say anything but Professor Michael closed his eyes and nodded his head at Arthur. Professor Michael then says to Judith pour me a glass of water dear will you and Judith got up and got it.

Arthur says me father who was Anthony's grandfather used get the exact same, used have terrible fits. Do you feel like your tongue is hard like a stone and you have a bolt of pain one ear to the other.

Professor Michael hummed in his glass, it meant yes.

And do you feel a bolt of pain in the spine of your back and a pain the back of the knees says Arthur.

Professor Michael swallowed his water sharp in his throat and hit the glass down on the table. Judith looked at him and put her hand on his arm.

Yes says Professor Michael.

Ah yes says Arthur. He says you have the look on your face the exact same me father used have the morning after one of his fits, the yellow above the eyes and the red in them and the grey below them and the white and blue lips and the red the sides of your mouth and the green the side of your head.

And you're saying you have these fits how many year, three four year.

They've been going on for about ten Michael isn't that it says Judith.

Ten I'd say he says.

Has it been the same level of bad through the whole of them ten year says Arthur.

Judith says what was it like in the early years Michael, bad wasn't it.

Bad says Professor Michael.

And he's been pinged from doctor to doctor in all that time and nobody can shed any light on what's wrong says Judith. She says to Professor Michael you've had every medicine and every test going haven't you Michael.

Oh no you don't want to be trying no doctors with that says Arthur. Me own father tried the doctors and none of them could cure him.

Was your father ever cured says Judith.

Yes he was miss yes he was says Arthur. There is only one cure for these fits and it's up the mountains you have to be going he says. One of the mornings after me father had a fit a man that we knew that was after calling around said he knew the cure and he brought me father up above to the mountains and on the bog the man found the things he was looking for, boiled them up, made the cure, and me father says the moment he took it he felt things was right in him. The man made him remember the things went in the cure said if ever he had a fit again he was to head up the mountains with someone and make up the cure from this but me father never had a fit again from that day. One drink of the cure was all was needed and the fits never came on him again, is true as anything, and this was a man didn't believe any of that thing, had all his faith in doctors and these men of the world.

Do you know what went into the cure says Judith.

Oh I do maam of course says Arthur, sure we was all made remember it including Anthony's father Aubrey. The twigs of the bog myrtle is the main part of it but there's other parts to it too but one thing you do need that is not on the bog is a tin pot or kettle.

Judith says almost jumping out her seat but sure we have a tin kettle.

I know maam sure I seen it in the room beside says Arthur.

Judith went in and got the kettle. It was a battered and ugly thing with a spout came out very long in a vicious beak.

Arthur says this is just the thing is needed.

Judith put her hand on Professor Michael's shoulder. She says what do you say Michael we have nothing to lose.

Professor Michael says I suppose not, I'm not feeling the best though.

She says Michael it'll be worth the effort if we can finally find a cure for this thing. What do you say fellas, would you be okay with that, if we went to the mountains, I mean I'll drive, and Arthur you could help us gather the ingredients up there on the bog.

Arthur says I'd be happy to help if the man is suffering maam, if I have the wisdom how to cure this thing I would feel bad keeping it and him sick there. Maam he says, can we take some of the small bits of wood I seen beside your fire place in the room.

Yes of course, and anything else you might need Judith says.

She went out with Professor Michael to the hall to gather themself, get their coats.

I looked at Arthur. He was looking at the wall, chewing a smile, his eyes bright and shining.

I says what's all this. I says is this tricks.

He moved his eyes but not his head to look at me. He says no tricks no.

Judith came back in the kitchen, she says Anthony you'll come with us yes.

Arthur says oh he'll come with us sure. He'll want to see how all this is done.

Judith's car was a silver Ford estate car, was twenty five year old she said. It was wrecked inside, it smelt of feet and old rain, and it was noisy when it was going. I sat in the front with Judith. I could not hear Arthur and Professor Michael in the back. There was a hissing and flapping over my head and I seen there was a hole in the roof, was covered in a sheet was stuck on with water proof tape said Judith. She said there used to be a sun roof where the hole was but it came off one time she was going a hundred mile an hour and it hit the car behind but she could not stop because she was breaking the law.

She says shouting behind to Arthur are we going in the right direction.

Arthur came forward his head on Judith's seat he says just keep going this way maam.

Out in front past the houses was the mountains and we kept in that direction. When we got to the bottom of the mountains Arthur came forward again he says maam you wouldn't mind stopping the car only I meant to go in the house before we left it.

Judith brought the car over the side of the road by a low wall and Arthur hopped over the wall.

All right in the rear there says Judith to Professor Michael.

Holding on my dear holding on says Professor Michael.

She watched Arthur concentrating behind the wall.

She says Anthony I hope you're getting something out of these nights in my house.

I says they're very good.

She says we're certainly getting a lot from you being there. You've enriched our group. Isn't that right big head she says to Professor Michael.

Oh very true says Professor Michael.

She says I just want you to know that we're all very keen that you and your uncle stay part of the group.

Thank you I says.

She watched Arthur climbing back over the wall she says we're both of us in our own way in the same boat.

Arthur got back in the car and Judith says I was just saying what crap society is Arthur aye.

Crap maam fucking shit says Arthur.

I looked at Professor Michael sitting beside him, he was looking out the window picking his teeth.

Turn your position to your advantage that's the way she says.

Professor Michael says let's turn this car to our advantage and be on our way dear.

Yes Michael says Judith. She says to Arthur will any of these hill sides around here do, they all look quite boggy.

Arthur says no miss you'd want to be going in a bit to the ground more open to the wind. Take the car over the hill and follow the road as it dips and goes by the side of the mountain.

When we went over the hill the colour of the ground changed, it was a browner colour, and we went down with the road and followed it along the side of a valley. We went into pine trees and out again and the wind hit the side of the car made it shake on the road and Arthur says stop it.

Right here Arthur says Judith.

Right here this is the exact spot you be wanting he says.

We got out the car the four of us.

Judith says to Professor Michael how are you feeling.

He stretched his arms wide he says much much better dear.

Arthur says are you right for the walk across the field sir.

I'm well up for it you might say he says.

I can't wait to see how this is done says Judith. She put her arms around Professor Michael's arms and squeezed him, she looked at him like an excited child.

We went off the road into the bog, Arthur leading the way. It was happy enough the start of it, Judith and Professor Michael were laughing about it, but soon we found the going was not easy. The ground was lumps and holes, you had to step on the lumps, sometimes your foot slid in a hole. Arthur was on ahead, it was like it was natural for him. He was like the tiny birds were darting and springing low over the ground. His hands were free but the rest of our hands were not free. I had in my hand the kettle, I had in the other hand a bag from Judith's house with a newspaper and a fire lighter in it. Judith had under her arms the shelfs the inside of her cooker, the bars of it. Sometimes she had a shelf under each of her arms, they looked like wings to keep her steady, sometimes she had both of the shelfs under one arm to free the other arm to help Professor Michael. Professor Michael found it the hardest, he was a big man with a big head and a lot of thick hair and he was not steady. He had over his shoulder a small bag with the wood in it. When Judith held him they did not help the other, they slipped. Someone seen the group of us they would have thought we were strange. They would have seen these people on the bog in the wind with these things of metal that were taken and these bags and their back crooked, they would have thought these people are escaping they have been moved on.

I seen Arthur was heading toward a small tree and when he got to the tree he stopped at it. I came to him I says are you trying to drown them. He said nothing he looked across at Judith and Professor Michael until they caught up to us. They were breathing hard but they did not give out, Judith had a big smile on her face but a purple and red face, Professor Michael had a yellow face.

Arthur had a twig of the tree in his hand he says this is it now see and he held it out. He says this is the bog myrtle one of the main ingredients of the cure for the fits. He twisted some more of it off the tree he says about this much.

Judith says and so we set up here and we boil this up do we.

Arthur says ah no maam like I says before the bog myrtle is one of the main ingredients but it's not the only thing in it, there's two other ingredients we need to get. The thing about it is where you find the last of the ingredients is where you must boil up the kettle see.

Of course says Judith.

Arthur says to Professor Michael are you happy to be going on now sir.

Very happy he says, let's proceed.

The next bit of the walk was beyond the tree up the mountain. When we got to where we thought was the top of the mountain there was more to go, it was up and up, was hard on the legs. There was a wind against us, there were small round creatures in the turf got stuck on your shoes and the bottom your trousers. I seen Arthur way ahead, head down. I looked back I seen Judith and Professor Michael swaying about like drunks. I could not see the road now, I could not see Judith's car. We'd walked two mile we must have done. I shouted up at Arthur but the wind was coming in rivers over the grass, splitting into streams saying whisht was the sound, blowing back the sound, this one moment the wind was a knife was cutting, was ice in the throat.

Arthur was leaned in low to the wind, he was a black animal. Then he straightened and he shouted, his voice came down the mountain with the wind. Same again, he stood on the spot didn't look at me when I came to him, he was looking down at Judith and Professor Michael. He had his hand in a fist to them, his hand streaked with turf, he waited until they came to him.

Roots he says to them.

Professor Michael had tears down his cheeks and his nose was streaming.

Judith says Arthur we can't do this for much longer.

Arthur says maam we must go on, there is the last ingredient still to get.

Judith says is it absolutely necessary that we come with you all the way.

It is maam it is says Arthur. Didn't I say to you we must boil up the medicine on the spot where we find the last ingredient he says.

Judith didn't say nothing, she looked back down the mountain over the bog then she says okay.

Then Arthur says this. He says maam what we'll do is you come to the top up there the three of you to the high ground, it isn't long to walk. You can wait there and rest and you can watch me, it's flat ground and wide ground there and you can see me from a distance. If I find the last bit of the cure I'll wave at you or ring you on me phone and you can come to me.

Before we went Arthur took the kettle from me, he put the twigs in it and the roots. He says this is the place to be filling the kettle with good rusty bog water, and he filled it from a spring in the ground.

Right let's move he says.

It was true what Arthur said, the highest ground was flat, but there didn't seem nowhere to sit, the ground was wet all about. All we could do was watch Arthur go away in the distance. Sometimes he would seem to go in the ground, sometimes he would leap about left and right. Then we seen him go down a while.

Professor Michael says something seems to be up.

After four five or ten minutes we did not know if he was in trouble or if he found the thing was needed for the cure. Then we seen his head rise. He was in a hole, we seen him come up he was scrambling. He stood on the ground and he waved, he whistled the sharp loud whistle he could do.

When we got to him we seen he been in a crater in the ground Professor Michael said, a wide hollow. Down in the bottom the crater was a dead sheep, a yellow dirty heap. Arthur had his coat off, he was holding it with one hand over his shoulder. His sleeve was rolled up on the arm he had loose. His arm to his elbow was streaked and dirty now with turf and something darker and dirtier. He had in his hand a bit of smooth red meat it looked, it was the sheep's heart.

Professor Michael says to Arthur we don't know how long that sheep has been dead for.

Arthur says it has not been dead long.

Judith says are you sure Arthur.

He says I am maam.

She says to Professor Michael well I suppose he will be boiling it.

Arthur says it is true I will be boiling it, it is part of the ingredients for this cure.

Now we moved about the crater to the other side of it where we could walk in it. We went in past the dead sheep, we looked at it each of us, we stood about it. The front of it was torn open. Professor Michael lifted the eyelid of it, he seemed happy with it.

Now we have all the things is needed Arthur says and he threw his coat on the ground.

He lifted the lid of the kettle, he pressed the heart in it, it went ploop in the water. He put the kettle down. He bent down and wiped his arm on the ground to clean it. I seen the tops of his trousers were bulging almost bursting, it looked wrong. He not only been scavenging for dead sheep he been looking for good sized stones he could make a fire with and putting the stones in his trousers. Not long then he had a fire built up on a cooker shelf on the ground out of a circle of stones and inside of the stones the newspaper packed in balls and the wood from Professor Michael's bag. He put the second cooker shelf on top of the stones, he put the kettle on the bars and he says now we wait until this boils up. He tapped the side of the kettle he says yes a good tin kettle. Then he picked up his coat from the ground and put it on him and he pulled the collar up about his chin.

Judith says to Professor Michael how are you feeling now.

He says I'm okay. He had his hands on his hips and he was moving his hips and waist about, it was to keep the blood moving. He says I feel like I'm back in the boy scouts.

The cold was bad and we moved in close around the fire, right up to it to get the heat. Our hands were in our pockets and our faces were nearly touching and under our chin the flames were licking up the sides of the kettle.

Do we know any songs says Judith. She looked at Arthur and at me.

Ding dang ding dang goo goo says Professor Michael.

I don't know songs I says.

The kettle bubbled and Arthur says she's singing now.

We stepped back from the fire and Arthur took off his coat one side of his body and pulled the sleeve the other side over his hand. He stooped down and took the handle of the kettle and lifted it.

Judith says has it boiled long enough Arthur.

Arthur says it has maam, the ingredients was well mixed. We only had to get it to a good heat.

Okay says Professor Michael. The side of his bag had a cup with a lid, he took this cup. Okay okay he says.

He held the cup out to Arthur. Arthur lifted the kettle to the cup and the cup was filled with steam and when the steam was gone dirty looking water was left.

So this is it says Professor Michael.

Arthur says take that now and if you're the same as me father you won't never be troubled with the fits again, they will be gone.

Okay so says Professor Michael. Bottoms up he says.

He sipped at it and made a shape with his mouth like he did not like it, mam mam he went with his mouth.

All in one go says Arthur.

It's very hot says Professor Michael.

Take your time with it says Arthur.

Professor Michael blew and sipped at it, blew and sipped at it.

Well done hun says Judith.

When it was nearly gone he looked in the end of the cup this not happy look on his face and he swirled the cup about.

Drink that bit of it too that is the good bit says Arthur.

In for the penny says Professor Michael and he knocked the rest of it back. Then he threw the cup at his bag and he lifted his face to the sky and he says agh.

Good says Arthur. Okay he says. Let's get back on the road.

Yes says Judith. She smiled.

Arthur put the kettle on the ground. He kicked off the top shelf of bars to the ground, kicked over the stones, kicked up the bottom shelf. He pressed the shelfs in the ground with his feet, he says you'll be wanting them again maam, leave them cool in the turf a minute.

Professor Michael made a noise, he was holding his stomach.

Judith says to him are you okay hun.

He did not look well. His face was tight, he was showing his teeth.

Arthur says that's the cure working. Leave it go down it'll be all right.

His face eased a bit.

Would you like a mint Michael says Judith.

Arthur says back at her don't give him nothing, let the cure settle will you. He looked at Professor Michael, nodding, then he looked back at Judith. What's bad is good for you isn't that it yes he says.

He turned around and lifted one of the shelfs from the ground. It dripped with slime and dirt, he held it away from him. He held it there watching the drips dropping one bar down to the next bar and down to the next. He was observing this. His face had a pained look. Then he said something not looking at anyone, he did not say it loud, it was the psalm a hundred and thirty that our people would say to help them-self and help others.

He says out of the depths I cry to you o Lord Lord hear my voice let your ears be attentive to my voice in suffocation.

He did not finish these words because Professor Michael looked like he was dying, he was on his knees. He was so bad he could not even scream.

Michael Michael says Judith.

This was not looking good, I seen it.

Oh Christ Michael Judith shouts and she beating his back.

I went up to him I says put him lying down.

He's not breathing says Judith.

He was a deep red colour in the face now, he looked the worst he looked all day.

Arthur took Judith by the shoulders. He threw her away, Professor Michael fell to the side.

Leave him lie there Anthony says Arthur.

What have you done shouts Judith, how dare you touch and shove me like that she shouts.

Let's see here Anthony says Arthur.

Professor Michael's body shook all a sudden, the whole of his body jumped an inch from the ground.

He's having a fit says Arthur.

You've poisoned him Judith screams that's what you've done she says, and she threw herself down between Arthur and Professor Michael. She tapped Professor Michael on the face she says Michael can you hear me Michael.

Settle woman says Arthur.

He's swallowed his tongue says Judith.

He has not swallowed his tongue he's having a fit says Arthur.

He has swallowed his tongue quick someone says Judith. She put her fingers in his mouth but Professor Michael bit her fingers and she screamed.

Arthur got the kettle he says to Judith move out the way.

What are you going to do with that she says.

Move out the way he says.

Professor Michael's head now was lying on a pillow of turf. Arthur moved the spout of the kettle against Professor Michael's lips and he moved it to get it in his mouth. He lifted the kettle and hot water came out the spout and ran over Professor Michael's lips and chin.

What are you doing to him says Judith.

Now Arthur stabbed the spout of the kettle in Professor Michael's mouth, he pushed it right in, he lifted the kettle right up. More hot water came pouring, filling Professor Michael's mouth, pouring out the sides. Professor Michael was not making any noise but the hot water was coming.

You beast you're killing him says Judith.

I wasn't sure neither, I didn't think this was the right way to be doing it, I says the same as Judith, I says to Arthur ease up ease up you're hurting him. I jumped at Arthur, I pulled him away from Professor Michael, pulled him on the ground with me.

Get off me boy he says.

Then we looked up and Professor Michael was spluttering, he was moaning, coughing. Slowly he stopped moaning, things were calm, he settled.

See maam says Arthur. He's all right, all I had to do was pull away his tongue.

Judith knelt on the ground beside Professor Michael. She had him sit up, she had her arm around him. She took out her phone and she pressed it. She looked angry at Arthur, took him in, waited for the person the other end to speak. Then she turned her eyes and then her head away and she spoke.

She says hello yes does this handle mountain rescue. Yes yes Dublin Wicklow mountain rescue.

She said to the man Professor Michael was sick and she needed to get him to a hospital quick.

Where are we she says to Arthur.

The mountains above Dublin he says.

Yes yes where exactly says Judith.

Tell the man you're not far from the mast of Kippure, you're to the west of it says Arthur.

He got up, he brushed his trousers. He walked over to Judith and Professor Michael.

Can I just say something he says.

Judith covered the phone with her hand. Go away now she says to Arthur.

Something quick he says.

Bye she says to the man on the phone.

Can I just say something quick maam, to you maam Arthur says.

I don't want to hear any more from you she says.

I went over too, I joined him.

Go away the both of you she says. You've done enough harm she says.

We sat down all of us on the wet dirty turf and we waited. No one cared about the wet, no one talked about anything. The light was dying. Judith was holding Professor Michael, petting him, thinking the helicopter will come soon we will be all right my lovely. Arthur was thinking about himself, I was not thinking about myself I was thinking about Arthur too. I looked at him his legs spread out in front of him, his bones going cold like mine, tense the feeling from the cold. His shoulders were down his head was down, his chest was heaving, he was in himself could be said, beaten he looked, stretched and laid out, but his guilt would keep him alive and ready, ready but no ideas now, no ideas.

I moved up to him, I slid my legs, my knuckles in the turf, I says quiet we're all right, we're all right. A laugh rose up through him like a bubble, shook his body, was gone. A noise came from the distance too, a roar and a rattle.

I thought about what trouble we could have been in, I thought about guards and helicopters. I seen spots of light in the air, discs. But I did not care about any trouble was the way I was feeling. I thought of him that other place the land was dead, the black wet land around those parts, that dead land one sunk lake one fallen mound two families called their home.

I says we are back in the country wha.

I seen it again. I seen it all and there we were. Three year before. Back. Three hundred year before, four hundred year, a thousand. Back the way it is back the way it should be. One body lowered in the ground among ten thousand more, a thousand people from two families stood above the soil, a thousand rusted rails loose in their hold. Many reasonable gentlemen telling us there will be no trouble, a priest fighting to be heard over a helicopter above. I seen the lump that Arthur threw in the air, I seen the height it got. I seen another lump in his hand, it was in his left hand. I seen his thumb that was his toe close in and his fingers tighten, the thumb and the fingers moving in a twisting natural movement like the petals of a flower twisting closing running away from each other but coming to meet in some way, I seen the lump turning to water and tiny grains and I heard the helicopter above.

And this is the way. It is funny, you would laugh. Professor Michael got lifted strapped to a man in the air by his arse. When he was in the helicopter the man in the strap came down again for Judith. The grass swirled, the hair on the sheep rose, the noise was fierce. The noise, and below it Arthur laughing, spitting now, the spit rolling across his face. The helicopter floated, Judith and Professor Michael in it, me and Arthur looking at its white and red belly. Then off it went, tipped to the side, gone. The hair on the sheep died down, the two of us, the three of us, here we were, there we were, all was quiet, nothing different only for the fire, we were stuck but what about it.

12

My father and Arthur did not get on. It was never the way. They thought different things, they lived lives that were different. The Cliffs was not a place I was brought. I was brought only the few times and my father did not like it. I ran wild there. I was with the other childer up among the rocks.

Arthur was Buck from The High Chapparal but I didn't know The High Chapparal. The High Chapparal was a cowboy film, I was Buck's friend.

We went one time in our van to help Arthur. Our grand little van my father sold the vegetables and the fountains from when I think about it now. I was ten maybe twelve and I could add numbers well and I wasn't bad with the words. We went because I said I wanted to go. My father respected education. My father always in a fit and always agitated and if I said something he listened in those moments.

Arthur had come in for some scrap from a factory had been cleaned out. He been promised it a long time and the fella dropped it himself in the lorry said it was no good to him. I remember it. Copper pipes and copper radiators, I remember helping to shift it to the back of the van. I remember it all because this was the day my father knew he was right in the way he was set. I remember the look on his face. What are you trying on was the look. It was in the feel of the radiators, the sound they made, the way the pipes packed into his hand. I do not want this was the look. I remember the look on Arthur's face, dismissive is the word, not looking my father straight, a mocking shake of the head, a sure this is the way these things operate, this is the way it's been done oh years filling old radiators and pipes with dirt to put extra weight on the scales in the yard. And my father with a turn of the head was a whisht was all, I don't want to be hearing none of it.

I remember the journey into Dublin, squeezed in beside Arthur on the passenger side, the cursing out of him. We'll be rich beyond our wildest fucking thoughts he says. In the van was the cross hanging from the mirror and the Blessed Mother above the glove box and the sticker of Padre Pio in the corner of the windscreen who my father did not yet think was the Devil's man in the field. He didn't like anyone other than himself cursing in front of them and he said to Arthur to hold his mouth.

The laughing out of Arthur is what I remember, saying the boy's heard worse out of you, and laughing until he was dried out, and quiet now the rest the way, and the directions shouted out like a dog next lights next lights, and my father not rising, gripping the wheel tight, his eyes on the road. And my father's head would not turn now for nothing until we got to that bridge in Dublin. I remember thinking he was going to say something to me, the way I seen him the side of my eye, and looking to see him looking past me, up the river. That's to where the new buildings are being built says Arthur. And sure that's the way, that's the way now he says.

The yard was not far on the other side. When we pulled in Arthur saluted a gentleman and pointed my father the way to the scales. The scales was a platform you drove your van on and they weighed your van with the scrap and then they took off the scrap and you came back and they weighed you again and you were paid for the weight of your scrap and your type of scrap. After we had ourself weighed my father drove us where the piles of scrap were lying on the ground. We got out the van and Arthur was muttering something about it was one of the young fellas we'd want to be getting and not the owner of the yard. But it was too late for that because the yard owner was coming over to us.

Arthur says to the yard owner how are you Larry I've some good stuff for you this time.

The yard owner did not say anything, he had his hands on his hips.

Arthur says to my father loud Larry here is from Kerry and Kerry are going great this year isn't that right Larry.

The yard owner did not pay heed to Arthur. He waved over for two of his lads. Right he says let's get it off.

Arthur and my father got up on the van and Arthur lifted a pipe and threw it on the ground.

You will pass each item along to my boys says the yard owner.

The first of these lads knew something was wrong from the first radiator he felt. He dropped it on the ground and he whistled to the yard owner. The yard owner made a sign to the lads and the two of them took the radiator to a shed and we heard cutting from the shed. Arthur and my father would not look the yard owner in the eye but I tried to look the yard owner in the eye but the yard owner was looking at Arthur and my father. Arthur seemed calm about it and my father to be fair to him there was no looking over at Arthur, we were stuck in it now all of us together.

The yard owner went in the shed and then he came back this concentrated look in his eyes. He said he'd give Arthur say eighty pound for the lot and though Arthur's scrap was worth more than that there was no argument out of Arthur because he knew he'd been found out with the dirt.

The yard owner says now clear the rest of it, so my father and Arthur took the last bits off the van. Then they got down to drive the van on the scales again.

Arthur turned to me he was almost crying. He says Anthony you have to get in with us to keep as much of the same weight we had before we took the scrap off.

I was about to climb in the van then the yard owner said something took us all out.

You fucking pack of thieves he says. Think I'm a fucking fool. You can get your van and hit the high way.

My father couldn't take none of that. He stood up to the yard owner he says now hang on there's no need to be speaking like that.

Fuck off out of here the yard owner says to my father.

Now whisht a while whisht a while says Arthur and he turned to my father like he was speaking to him as much and he went back to the yard owner and says like the man says there's no place for language like that Larry and you don't want to be jeopardising our partnership because I been good to you these years and I got plenty more good stuff good quality copper lead aluminium.

Says the yard owner I don't want it he says, I'm selling up in three months. Think scrap is worth fuck to me it's land is where the money is.

Well Arthur let it fly he says what kind of a person are you to take the scrap off us at all and you having done a deal with someone to sell the land it makes me sick.

That's it says the yard owner you talk yourself into getting nothing off me, go on, go on.

Arthur could say no more, his face was sweating. He turned to my father he was fuming. He turned back to the yard owner he spat on the ground between them.

Fine says the yard owner, and he reached in his pocket took his wallet out, took four twenties out, threw the money where the spit was, and Arthur in an instant stooped to take it.

My father coughed, he bent down quick, put his hand on Arthur's shoulder. Arthur knew what my father meant by this, he froze there.

The yard owner started laughing, his eyes wrinkled up.

Fucking bloody eejits he says. Come on boys he shouts to his lads, and the three of them went back in their hut and the lads were laughing too.

Then my father eased his hand off Arthur's shoulder and Arthur went forward slow and picked the money off the ground. And then we all picked ourself up was what we did because pick ourself up was what we had to do. We drove out the place and we were a very different mood to the mood we were driving in it except for my father who was sure now very sure.

Arthur shook his head. He could not understand what was after happening, he could not take it in. He said the trick filling the radiators was normal.

He says I been found out the once or twice I'll say that to you right, I'll say that, but I always been able to get back with Larry, always. I do not understand it I just do not he says.

He said the man depended on him as much as he the man.

I feel betrayed I do he says. Let me tell you a story he says.

My father said he didn't want to be hearing none of his stories.

Just to make the point Arthur says.

I've had enough of stories my father says.

Listen to me says Arthur.

My father hit on the brakes.

No you listen to me he says. Get out the van. You've made a fool of us today and you're setting a bad example to Anthony.

Arthur started laughing but my father lifted the fist to him he says serious now Arthur I'm serious.

Arthur kept the trace of a smile on him, his face could not drop further, but he could not believe this and I could not believe this.

He says will you start up again and don't be getting mad.

My father tightened his fist he says to me Anthony cover your ears.

Arthur would not budge he says what's got in you Aubrey.

Right my father says and he got out the van and he went around the front of it. Arthur pressed the lock on the passenger door but my father didn't even try the handle. He started thumping the door, beating it with his fist, kicking it wild. The cross on the mirror swung, the Blessed Mother shook, and Arthur's reaction was to lift his arm to protect his head.

Get out get out get out my father screams.

Hold it hold it Arthur says. Look it, calm. I'm opening the lock. I'm getting out see he says.

He jumped on the ground. My father was stood on the spot, cooling, breathing. Arthur went past him and looked quick at his back.

He says for Jesus, wha. He shuffled off to the side the big lump of him, toward a wall, going in no direction, hoping my father would say get back in come on.

But my father would not say this, he would not say anything. He started up the van again. I looked out the passenger window, I seen Arthur stood his back to the wall, looking at us move away slow.

We drove on by the river, walls on our right the water on our left. We were driving on cobbles and the suspension on the van was broke and I could feel every cobble under us. Ahead of us were the taller buildings in Dublin.

My father looked up in his mirror. Look at him fucking scavenger he says.

I says why you want to be going in Dublin father and not going for the bridge. Father you're not going to leave Arthur now and no way of him getting back home I says.

He looked in the mirror again he says he has his eighty pound he can get home.

I says why you shout at Arthur and why you leaving him left like this.

I don't want him around no more says my father. He is bad for you Anthony he says.

Father this is not the way I says.

Anthony shush now he says.

Father I says. Listen now father I says.

The van slowed and slowed, my father's foot weaker on the pedal the further he got and his eyes falling to the road in front and then to nothing until he stopped.

And he gripped the wheel tight and his head came forward. And the cross on the mirror came to rest and the sea gulls screeked outside.

I says father.

And fuck it he says and he brought the van around in a U turn.

And there was Arthur on ahead, back to us, walking on, his head down checking the ground, scanning it for what could be got.

13

First thing Arthur did when we got back to Judith's silver Ford estate car was check the tail gate. He got down on his haunches, he put his hand below the window. The tail gate was open a crack and he looked in the crack. He jammed the tail gate up and down.

He says this thing was rattling on the way I thought it could be opened.

He took a stone from the ground and he went around the side of the car. He smashed the window on the driver's side, he opened the door and he got in.

He says are you not getting in.

I says is there glass.

He says a bit but it's all on my side.

We drove up the road the way we came all them hours before, we turned left and drove over the high part of the mountains again. We dropped down taking the road skirting the mountain sides. In the light of the headlamps I seen the brown bog turned to gorse and trees. Houses and the city of Dublin was on our left. There was a sign ahead pointing the way to Dublin down another road. When we came to the sign Arthur stopped the car, pulled it over to the side.

He had his sleeves rolled up. He looked desperate, filth all over him.

I says everything all right with you.

You can walk it from here he says.

I says what.

It's not far to your father's house he says, it's three mile or so it's all down the hill.

I says I am not going back to me father's house. Sure it's dark now.

You'll be all right once you get to the first houses down the hill he says.

Why don't you drive me down I says.

I can't he says.

Why not I says.

I can't go back anywhere near Dublin he says.

Why can't you I says.

Psychological he says.

What would you know about psychological I says.

I can't Anthony he says. They'll be after me sure. Go on now. Get back to your father's place. That is your place, your father is dying he says.

Would you fuck off out of it I says me father is not dying.

He is says Arthur.

Serious I says.

Not dying dying he says.

Fuck off I says.

He's dying on his own, things is getting in on him Arthur says. That is your place.

That's not me place I says.

That house in Dublin's not your place that is an awful place he says.

You liked it long enough I says.

Long enough he says.

I says you owe me rent for it.

Go on he says.

I looked down at Dublin. It was black and orange and there was a sea haze or smoke on it. The lights of it were shaking. Two white lights on two tall chimneys in the bay were blinking. Two red lights on a plane in the sky were blinking too.

I says where you going to go.

Off he says.

Off I says.

Off away he says.

Are you taking this car I says.

Don't be telling no one about this car he says.

What kind of place is away I says.

It's a place I seen clear in me head just recent he says.

England I says.

Maybe England he says.

Canada I says.

Maybe there too he says.

I got out the car I closed the door. I went around his side and put my face to the broken window.

Right I says to him. Well fuck off away so.

He looked at me, then he looked ahead of him. I stood up, stood back into the middle of the road, and the car went off, on, away.

14

My mother's father, one of the big Gillaroos, proved himself a decent man coming to our house and telling us all that he knew, the things that he heard. Here it is another story about the Sonaghans and the Gillaroos, the bones and the rest of it. Happened not long ago.

A year on from my trip to the Gillaroos another Sonaghan came through that hotel near Rath I stayed in. He was looking for the same things I was, could be said. He was looking to make the peace, but he was looking for one person. He came down because of a wedding. The wedding was on the next day but when he came into Rath he seen the party was already started. The chippers were full and the people were spilling into the street and the pubs were full too and the one or two country pubs were deserted. The person to ask about things was a country person but the country people had left the town these few days, there were none of them left in the town. The person to ask now was a guard so he went up to a guard, there were plenty of them in the town. He says to the guard where is the bride staying tonight and the guard said to him the Wu Tang Park Hotel.

The hotel car park was full of cars and the bar in the hotel was full of people. Every Gillaroo by the look of it was back in Rath the few days and it seemed a lot of them were following the bride. The man thought if he stayed in the bar long enough he would see the bride. This is what he did.

He was nervous about it to begin, he was sitting in the wasps' nest, a Sonaghan man, and he thinks to himself I cannot relax. He kept his left hand in his pocket or by his side, he kept it in a tight fist, his fingers over his thumb. After two pints though his head started to relax, he thought kind thoughts. He looked about him he thought it was a fine bar and a fine hotel, a great thing indeed that people like themself could build a place like this for themself where they could sit and enjoy a drink. The evening went on he even got relaxed enough he could talk to others. He went to the bar and he hit a fella on the shoulder, he did not mean it, he fell into him, but anyhows the end of it was the fella says to him come and join us for the cards. The next couple of hours so he sat with a group of them were playing cards. The thing about it was the more he played the cards the more concentrated he became in the cards and it sobered him a bit what it did, because the effect of it was he did not go to the bar again the whole time, he did not want anyone pulling tricks on him. The others playing were just as concentrated, their head was down, everyone was in it to win. They were playing more serious, the money in the pot was getting bigger and bigger, then all a sudden a noise started the other side of the bar. It was a whoop, a screek, and people were clapping their hands. The man looked up from his cards he seen the others in the group standing up out their seat and looking toward the end of the bar. He got up too he seen everyone was standing clapping their hands and whooping. They were all looking at the person he came to Rath to see, the beautiful bride he thought as he seen her.

After he seen her and everyone settled back in their seat he could not concentrate on the cards no more, he could not concentrate on anything. He heard one of the lads in the group say the Missy Elliott suite in the hotel was the best room in the hotel and that was where the bride was staying on her own this night. He asked one of the lads where the Missy Elliott suite was. The lad says on the second floor down the end of the hotel. He says to the group lads are we playing the cards the whole night I want to be meeting the others. The other lads in the group says we'll be winding down soon, then they looked at him they says are you all right, he says I'm not all right lads I think I'm going to give up. He got up from his seat he went over to the bar. He wanted to talk to the bride but he did not, he got nerves or he got sense. He got a drink anyhows and he stayed at the bar keeping an eye on the bride. He stayed there a good while. He said to himself if anyone asked him he would say his name was Pat Gillaroo from Glasgow but no one asked him. He drank three pints standing there at the bar but he left the fourth pint abandoned because he seen the bride moving off with her mother to more whooping and kissing. She went off out the door that she came in and the toilets were out that way too so he made like to go to the toilets. He seen the bride and her mother go in the lift. He ran up the stair, he ran fast, but he felt sick. When he got to the landing on the first floor he did get sick, he went on the window ledge. Then he walked the stair to the second floor slow. At the landing there he heard voices in the corridor. He looked careful round the door, he seen the bride and her mother hugging each other. They were down the end of the corridor outside the door of a room there.

He walked heavy down the stair holding the rail. He drifted out the hotel not looking back, he was like a zombie. He planned to come back but. He just wanted time to think things on his own, time to sober up some more. He went to his van and drove off in the direction away from Rath and into the dark. He was not too steady on the road because the drink was still in him. He slid all over the road. He did not get two hundred yard and he ended up his van in a ditch. He was shook but he was okay but his van was not, his van was stuck and it would not be coming out that ditch. But this moment he did not care about these things. Last thing he did before he got out his van was he looked over his shoulder and he seen his tool box opened and his tools spilt everywhere. He found his hatchet lying on the back of his seat and he put it inside his coat. Then he scrambled out the ditch the field side of it. He walked about the field in the dark in the moon, the last of the drink leaving him but a kind of madness taking hold. He found the gate of the field and an owl flew off the gate and he walked back on the road but he did not walk back in the direction the hotel, he walked away up the road in the dark breathing deep breathing out, sometimes shaking his head in his hands. He was an hour on the road, then he walked back in the direction the hotel.

When he got near the hotel he heard rap music coming over the fields. When he was outside the hotel the rap music was very loud and the windows of the bar were flashing with red lights. When he got in the hotel the rap music was so loud he would not have heard himself think if he was thinking but he was not thinking. He moved through the people in the bar, some of them dancing some of them lying across tables drunk, but no one seen him. He went through and out the other side and this time he got the lift to the second floor. He went down the corridor and he stood outside the door of the bride's room. His breathing was settled now and his head was calm but something was beating hard. It was the music up through the floor was beating hard he told himself. He knocked on the door but the knock was too gentle. He seen the eye hole in the door and he pressed his thumb against it and he knocked again louder.

Who's this comes the voice the other side of the door.

He knocked on the door again he says someone here has to talk to you.

The door began to open and he put his foot down the bottom of it to wedge it. He pushed it the full way. He took a step in the room and he shut the door behind him.

Arthur says the bride.

It is me Teresa hello he says.

Teresa was panicked. Her throat was tight she could not scream. Even if she could scream the music was too loud no one would have heard.

Teresa I've come back says Arthur. I've come back for you he says.

Get out this room says Teresa.

I been in torment Teresa without you says Arthur. I been risking my life sitting in that bar because of you and I don't care if I'm killed he says.

Arthur get out says Teresa.

Listen listen me Teresa please says Arthur. I been beating the roads of England and Germany thinking about you, I been beating me head. I could not take it no longer darling beautiful girl. I heard you were getting married to your own and I could not take it, I had to turn around.

Teresa was crying. Her breathing was a whistle she was panicked so much.

Don't be crying girl says Arthur and he took a step toward her his hand out.

Don't don't she says shaking her head.

Arthur says you cannot marry that man Teresa, there isn't no reason to be marrying that man. There isn't no reason you shouldn't be with me Teresa Teresa listen me listen me. There isn't no reason Teresa. Isn't no reason me name should bother anyone any side. We are all the same people Teresa, we come from the same. Don't be listening to no one.

Arthur's eyes filled up with tears themself. His voice was paining him. He held up his left hand and stuck out his thumb.

It's just skin is all he says. Lines on a hand. Nothing but. Caused trouble too long he says.

He took the hatchet out his coat.

Does me name bother you Teresa he says. Answer me yourself now darling don't be thinking of no one he says.

Teresa could not speak, she was stood with her back against the wall terrified looking at the hatchet.

Teresa I love you darling he says. He says do you know how much I love you darling.

He says do you.

I'll show you he says.

He walked over to the bed. He put his left hand flat on the rest at the end of it. He brought his hatchet down on his thumb and he cut the skin and broke the bone above the bottom joint.

He did not scream, Teresa did not scream.

He brought the hatchet down again, a fierce concentration in his eyes, in his head, and the thumb came off neat at the crack.

There was blood on the sheets of the bed, blood all over them. Arthur stepped back from the bed, he stumbled. He held his wrist, he squeezed it, but his eyes were looking fixed ahead at Teresa, caught Teresa's eyes. Teresa looked back in Arthur's eyes, she could not look at the bed and the blood. The music beating into the room now from below was like the beat of a heart for both of them. Things were slowed. But then the beat of Arthur's heart went slower than the beat of the music. He seen Teresa jump away from the wall and run past him. He turned and he seen her run out the room. He squeezed his wrist tighter. He went after her but he could not run. His right hand was losing its power, its grip on his wrist was weakening. He stumbled out the room, he stumbled down the corridor. He took two steps down the stair and he fell. He rolled down the stair to the feet of a group of fellas coming the other way.

This is Arthur Sonaghan they says. What'll we do with him.

Like many the men of our people his age my mother's father wears a hat and when he is inside commiserating he takes the hat off and holds it in his hands and when it is time to go he gets up from his seat and flicks the inside of it with his hand to open it out.

Only some things is certain about the story. Certain is Arthur turned up in Rath the night before Teresa Gillaroo's wedding, he went to the bar of the hotel, he played cards, he left the hotel, his van was found in a ditch, he went to Teresa's room, he cut off his thumb, he was found. Some lads brought him to the hospital but the doctors said they couldn't do nothing so he was taken to Dublin where the doctors could make thumbs out of toes. Certain too is no one will know the full truth of it all. Certain things about what happened Arthur, what he did on this night, nobody now living will ever know. The one person who knew the full truth isn't around to be asked no more, he is dead. That is what everyone thinks. You hope and some of us pray, but everyone thinks this.

Two weeks after I last seen Arthur on the road in the Dublin and Wicklow mountains Judith's silver Ford estate car was found in the sea off the end of a pier in the south of county Wexford and the car was empty. No body was found.

Says my mother's father but he was a wild unpredictable man, remember how he threw the stone at the helicopter at poor Aaron's funeral. His whole life, his whole wild deeds, was all leading to this.

True I says.

But he says. If there is some good, look at us now together in this house he says.

Yes I says to him. That is true too I says.

My mother's father did not stay long in our house. He felt strange being there and he was right to feel strange.

He says tell your father I came up when he gets back will you. And if there's anything I can do for you before I go let me know he says.

He was nearly at the door and I says to him there is Pap yes. There is one thing you can do I says.

Oh he says.

You can leave a message with me mother I says.

Of course I will Anthony anything at all I'll tell her for you he says. What is it.

Could I read you a letter I says.

I suppose you could Anthony yes if you like he says.

I will get it now I says.

Go and get it do he says.

This letter I kept under a jug in the television room. I brought the letter and the jug to the kitchen to my mother's father. It is not called a jug it is called an urn, it is white and gold with a rainbow shine on it. It is not a Christian thing. I set the urn in front of my mother's father on the kitchen table.

Before I read from the letter I said to my mother's father one last thing.

I says my father turned out to have a very good way with words.

15

Sometimes I think God and Arthur are cruel in their thoughts and actions because I am back in this house I grew up as a child. Arthur told me to go here and God is keeping me here. God is hoping I will learn something here. My father learnt to read and write and he went great, he learnt so he could read God's words but then he turned away from God and now God is being cruel. Arthur is laughing, and Arthur and Aubrey and Aaron are the flies between the curtain and the window.

The day after I found my father dead in his bed I found pearl and wood and metal burnt in a pile in a fountain, they were from crosses and pictures. There was sharp glass all over the ground. The week later I got rid of the rest of it. I went at it, cleaned the house out, I used my father's car to get to the dump. I stripped the paper from the walls, took up the carpet in my father's room. I bought tins of paint, I painted the whole house top to bottom. I threw Waterford Crystal at the wall, I brought the foreign man with the nerves burnt in the rain out to the wall, that was a man I was not expecting, I'd forgot about him. I broke up my father's bed, I brought that to the dump too. I threw the wood of it in the ground, nearly fell in the hole myself, could have been a funny thing. I put Eoin O'Duffy's bone in the bin. I caught a squirrel in the attic. When it was all finished I did not think I was finished. I did not know what to think.

Another day Mister FX came to the house. I was sitting my hands on my knees thinking what to do and I seen him come in the gate. I said to him my father was not in the house. Maybe I am a bad man for saying this. I thought for two seconds I might get a strange joy not saying to Mister FX about my father. Mister FX said it was a pity my father wasn't in the house because he wanted to make up with him.

Your father and I had a falling out some weeks ago about some very fundamental things and I regret that he says. It's gone on long enough now this stand off.

I was bringing trouble on myself, I knew it. Mister FX would be back and I would have to be straight with him. My father done the worst thing by a Christian man like yourself I would have to say to Mister FX. But I do not believe that, no I don't believe any of it, I would be straight with him. I do not believe like my father did not believe. He had no faith in the end he wrote. He did not know what was meant. But Mister FX did not come back, I must have made him afeard.

I do not know what is meant neither, I only know what my life is now. It is not one thing it is not the other. It is a life of waiting what it is. When you are not moving, when you are not settled, you are waiting. You are watching. But you learn out of it. You learn many things from getting bored. You learn about yourself you do. You learn there are others are bored, people in houses all about. I learnt there were many others in that tall old house in the city of Dublin I lived in were bored the same as me. They didn't know what to be doing with themself. I learnt there was one person in the house not keeping with the rules of the house, he was lonely and he needed a friend. How I knew was this. I was sitting in my seat. I was bored many nights in that house was the truth. I was thinking is this it, I may well been thinking this very thing. In my seat, my seat been there all I knew the life of the building. I was saying to myself these questions. What was I thinking and is this it. Is this what people do. And I heard this noise. I heard a tapping on the floor outside, a steady tip tip sound on the wood. First I thought it was rats then I knew it was a dog. I thought he might go away but he kept moving backward and forward on my bit of the landing. I could tell he was a big dog by the sound of him. He was panting with the movement like he was a heavy thing and the movement was slow though I could tell it was quick as he was able. Sounded like he was in a panic indeed. I heard him go down the stair and I thought that would be him gone. But then he leapt back up and I heard him again scratching on the bit of the landing then he went again down the stair then he came up all the way. He could not decide in his head. I heard him move right up to my door and I could hear him breathe down by the gap at the bottom pushing his nose right in. I could tell he was a very big dog now this point. The door was knocking in the frame. Then I heard him move away so I got up. I opened the door and he was moving for the door the other end and he turned soon as I opened my own door. I says how do you do to him I says. He was frozen there now curled about toward me. He was expecting a man but not that one was the thing. I took my seat and I put it beside the head of my bed so I was sitting looking out the door at him. That put him at ease. I could see the stress go out his face if that is possible. He came toward me his tail lifted and his head swinging from his collar, this easy stride on him now. I do not need to look you in the eye as I walk he was saying to me because you are now on my level was what he was saying. He came in my room and the top of his head sailed in kissed my knee is how I would put it. He was a big dog but a thin one only for a ring of fat that slid over his ribs when he moved. I patted his side and felt his ribs jump away. I thumped his back. I put my fingers in his ears and they smelt of biscuits. I left him at my seat with his tail moving slow side to side and I went to my fridge. All I had in it was some ham melted to water and some chocolate and I knew it was true that chocolate can kill a dog because I heard of it of one that that happened to. So I had a candle that was made of fat and I gave him that. I let him smell it first then he took it. I was surprised but I must have been expecting it to begin. I rubbed his head as he ate it. His hair was very smooth and it shined. You do feel sometimes that these big dogs like a firm handling. That hollow sound off them and the muscles going behind his jaw. Good lad I says to him. It did me good. And then he was gone too.

Thanks to the following: my brilliant agent Will Francis, and his fellow Janklovian PJ Mark. Clare Reihill, Olly Rowse and Nick Pearson at Fourth Estate, for their belief and guidance and for seeing this through. Mitzi Angel at Faber US, for the same. James Ryan, Éilís Ní Dhuibhne, Catherine Heaney, Niall Crowley, Treasa Coady, Niall McMonagle, Seamus Hosey, Lorelei Harris, Jesper Bergmann, Sean O'Reilly and Declan Meade, for their help. Paul Lynch, for the right words at the right time. My mother Anne, my sisters Ciara and Orla, my brother Ronan and my uncle Colin. And Jennifer, for her love and support and for coming back from America with me.

Thanks to the following: my brilliant agent Will Francis, and his fellow Janklovian PJ Mark. Clare Reihill, Olly Rowse and Nick Pearson at Fourth Estate, for their belief and guidance and for seeing this through. Mitzi Angel at Faber US, for the same. James Ryan, Éilís Ní Dhuibhne, Catherine Heaney, Niall Crowley, Treasa Coady, Niall McMonagle, Seamus Hosey, Lorelei Harris, Jesper Bergmann, Sean O'Reilly and Declan Meade, for their help. Paul Lynch, for the right words at the right time. My mother Anne, my sisters Ciara and Orla, my brother Ronan and my uncle Colin. And Jennifer, for her love and support and for coming back from America with me.